MURDER AT THE REGATTA

DAWN BROOKES

Storm

This is a work of fiction. Names, characters, businesses, places, events and incidents are either the products of the author's imagination or used in a fictitious manner. Any resemblance to actual persons, living or dead, or actual events is purely coincidental.

Copyright © Dawn Brookes, 2024, 2025

The moral right of the author has been asserted.

Previously published in 2024 by Oakwood Publishing.

All rights reserved. No part of this book may be reproduced or used in any manner without the prior written permission of the copyright owner. This prohibition includes, but is not limited to, any reproduction or use for the purpose of training artificial intelligence technologies or systems.

To request permissions, contact the publisher at rights@stormpublishing.co

Ebook ISBN: 978-1-80508-945-2
Paperback ISBN: 978-1-80508-946-9

Cover design: Emily Courdelle
Cover images: Shutterstock

Published by Storm Publishing.
For further information, visit:
www.stormpublishing.co

ALSO BY DAWN BROOKES

Lady Marjorie Snellthorpe Mysteries

Murder at the Opera House
Murder in the Highlands
Murder at the Christmas Market
Murder at a Wimbledon Mansion
Murder in a Care Home

Death of a Blogger (prequel novella)

Rachel Prince Mysteries

A Cruise to Murder
Deadly Cruise
Killer Cruise
Dying to Cruise
A Christmas Cruise Murder
Murderous Cruise Habit
Honeymoon Cruise Murder
A Murder Mystery Cruise
Hazardous Cruise
Captain's Dinner Cruise Murder
Corporate Cruise Murder
Treacherous Cruise Flirtation
Toxic Cruise Cocktail

Carlos Jacobi PI

Body in the Woods

The Bradgate Park Murders

The Museum Murders

Memoirs

Hurry up Nurse: Memoirs of nurse training in the 1970s

Hurry up Nurse 2: London calling

Hurry up Nurse 3: More adventures in the life of a student nurse

ONE

"Hang on, you lot. I can't keep up."

Marjorie Snellthorpe turned around to see Edna Parkinton lagging behind, every breath being forced in and out and sounding like a steam engine. "Why does she insist on wearing such high heels to something like this?"

Horace chuckled. "You know our Edna, she likes to dress for the occasion and believe me, she won't be the only one."

Marjorie did know Edna, and that was part of the trouble. Her cousin-in-law always drew attention to herself wherever they went. In between stopping to catch her breath, she was waddling like an oversized duck.

"She told me she's hoping to meet a millionaire with a yacht," said Frederick, a light twinkle in his eyes. His and Edna's relationship was often tense, to say the least, as Edna didn't have the patience for Frederick's mild manner. Sneaky, Edna called it, but Marjorie was fond of Frederick and well aware that her cousin-in-law made him nervous, bringing out the worst side of his insecurities.

Edna finally caught up with them. "What's the hurry, anyway? It's not as though we're late, is it?"

"Horace wants to arrive early before the crowds amass. I expect this way we'll get a better view of the races," said Marjorie. "It's kind of him to bring us, so the least we can do is be there at the time he suggests."

The four friends had arrived in the historic town of Henley-on-Thames the day before and Marjorie was already sensing the occasion that the royal regatta brought to the place, with early attendees visible in the distance. Although the shops were closed at this time in the morning, their frontages displayed the uniqueness only found in small towns these days.

"I don't understand why you've got this thing on your bucket list, Marge. A load of boats racing up and down the Thames is not my idea of fun... Let alone six days of it!"

"Then why are you here?" Marjorie muttered under her breath. Although she knew why. Edna hated to feel she was missing out and, on the whole, the four of them enjoyed each other's company, as long as Edna didn't send Frederick into a tizzy.

"Come on, old girl, think of the champagne."

Horace's comment got the desired response: a beaming smile. "Now you're talking. Come on then, what are we waiting for?"

You, thought Marjorie, but said, "If you're quite ready."

"Here, Edna, take my arm. You're lucky it's not rained for a week, otherwise we'd be spending the day digging your heels out of the mud."

Edna took Horace's proffered arm. "You told me it was formal attire in the Stewards' Enclosure. Men in blazers and women in dresses below the knee or suits and whatnot. I'm just doing as instructed. I bought this dress and shoes especially. And you won't believe how much this hat cost. A bloomin' fortune."

Marjorie had to agree with Horace. Edna was certainly dressed for the occasion: a pink and blue floral dress with white high-heeled sandals that made her totter like someone trying to cross a tightrope. The new sky-blue hat matched the flowers on her dress.

"I don't remember seeing that hairstyle before," Marjorie said.

"I'm pleased you noticed, Marge. Horace bought me a new one. He thought it would be ideal for the occasion." Edna patted the latest acquisition in her wig collection: a black bobbed style that wouldn't look out of place if she disembarked from one of the many moored luxury boats they'd passed the evening before when they had taken a walk by the river. Henley was renowned for its boating community and its history. Many of the boats were residential and Marjorie had enjoyed the floral displays and bright patterns that marked them out. It had been a visual treat.

"The hair suits you," said Marjorie, grateful Edna wasn't wearing one of her more outrageous wigs. Edna had suffered permanent alopecia following cancer chemotherapy a few years before and managed the psychological aspects of the condition by changing her hairstyle, colour and length almost as often as Marjorie changed her clothes.

While Horace and Edna took the lead, Marjorie waited for Frederick. "Are you looking forward to the regatta?" she asked.

"I was until Horace showed up in his striped blazer looking like a part of the scenery. I don't have as many suits as I used to, and certainly nothing like that."

Marjorie looked from Horace's blue and white striped blazer, beige flannel trousers and boater hat with a light blue ribbon around it, to Frederick's checked shirt and mismatched tie under his unbuttoned brown jacket. He sensibly wore a brown trilby to protect his bald head from the blazing sun that was forecast for later in the day. Fashionable dress sense wasn't Frederick's forte, but what he wore always looked good enough on him and his shirts were a part of who he was. Even Edna didn't criticise Frederick's choice of clothing, perhaps understanding that he didn't like to waste money on what he considered unimportant.

"Horace will always go the extra mile. We're only getting inside the Stewards' Enclosure because he's a member. Perhaps it's what members are required to wear."

"Hmm, well, he didn't mention it in the dos and don'ts yesterday. Maybe he's just an exhibitionist."

Frederick was right. Horace could be a show-off, but a decent one with a generous spirit to whom nothing was too much trouble.

"What are you two talking about back there?" called Edna as they joined a queue of people waiting for the gates to open. A crowd had already assembled to enjoy breakfast in Little Lion Meadow, advertised as a meeting place for people to gather before entering, and the buzz in the air could be felt as well as heard.

"We were admiring Horace's blazer," said Marjorie.

"Thank you," said Horace. "I used to row a bit myself back in the day—"

"Of course you did," Frederick muttered.

"—but mostly, I entertained corporates here during the regatta week."

Edna nudged him. "Stop bragging, Horace."

"I'm not bragging. I'm merely stating the facts."

"I'm surprised you haven't been here before, Marge. Looking around, it's your sort of thing."

"It's one of those experiences that Ralph and I never got around to..." *Like far-flung cruises, the Trans-Siberian railway, and the Orient Express.* Memories of the many things she and Ralph had planned to do when he retired flooded Marjorie's mind, the problem being that Ralph had never really retired, and then he had died suddenly, leaving her to live their shared dreams on her own. In that, she and Edna had something in common. Edna's husband had died while they were planning to travel the world. At least Marjorie and Ralph had enjoyed several cruises, which had left her with fond memories.

Her widow's life had vastly improved since she'd met her close friend Rachel Prince, who she looked upon as the granddaughter she'd never had, and had got even better since her three octogenarian friends had come into it. They might not agree on everything, but they were always keen to try new things and mostly understood each other. And apart from a few murders along the way, they were all enjoying their ninth decade.

"At least we're doing it now," said Frederick, offering Marjorie a reassuring look. "It's my first time at the Henley Royal Regatta too."

Edna couldn't suppress an eye roll. "Yeah, but that's no surprise. You aren't as grand as *Lady* Marjorie Snellthorpe" – Edna's use of her full name and title was meant to be sarcastic – "you were just a plain old pharmacist."

Thankfully, the queue started moving before Marjorie leaped to Frederick's defence with something like *as opposed to being a lounge singer*, which would have led to Edna being offended. Edna could dish it out, but she couldn't always take the insults.

"Play nicely, Edna," Horace said, propelling her forwards. Horace handled Edna in a way that brought her in line, which was more than anyone else could do. Another reason he was a valued member of their quartet.

TWO

They arrived at the entrance to the Stewards' Enclosure, where Horace showed his membership card and their tickets, and they were soon being ushered into an expansive area with lush freshly mown grass. With the current heatwave hitting the south of England, Marjorie sensed a lot of work had gone into keeping the grass from drying out. Numerous tents and marquees were in place, serving a variety of drinks, food, and snacks. White picket fencing separated the hospitality tents and gardens from the rest of the enclosure and the pergolas were decorated with roses, clematis, and honeysuckle. The scent was divine. Food aromas also hung in the air, along with the whiff of freshly ground coffee. Marjorie was receiving an olfactory treat.

"There's our first stop," said Edna, inclining her head towards a sign saying COFFEE AND ICES. "I could kill for a strong coffee after all that walking."

Marjorie didn't point out that the walk had been less than half a mile from the hotel. It was often better to ignore Edna's exaggerated statements unless it was necessary to challenge them. Frederick cleared his throat as if about to do so, but swallowed hard instead, changing his mind.

It wasn't easy staying together as they weaved their way through the excitable crowds. Peals of laughter broke out all around the enclosure, but people appeared polite and friendly, stepping aside to allow others through when necessary.

Pleased Edna would not begin the day with a champagne breakfast, Marjorie said, "I hope they serve tea as well as coffee."

"I'm sure they will, Marge." Ignoring all etiquette, Edna moved swiftly to the garden outside of the tent, commandeering a table another group of people moving at a more leisurely pace was about to take. Edna on a mission was not to be deterred, and the people politely walked away. Astonished, but not surprised, Marjorie mouthed her apologies but the group didn't seem concerned.

Marjorie found the plastic seats comfortable enough but would have preferred them with padding. She wondered if the shop sold cushions. If not, the regatta might be a less enjoyable experience than she'd been hoping for. As she was only just over five-foot tall, the depth of most chairs made it difficult for Marjorie to shift into a position where her feet touched the ground. Horace must have noticed her wriggling in her seat.

"Don't worry, Marjorie. I've booked us front row canvas deckchairs by the river for when we're ready to watch the racing. And the seats in the grandstand all have cushions."

"Thank you. That's good to know." The enclosure was getting busier by the minute, and she could see why Horace had encouraged them to get there so early.

"See, Marge. It's a good job I made an effort. Look at some of those dresses. There's a lot of wealth here, by the looks of things."

Marjorie was indeed looking at the wonderful summer dresses and suits worn by the women, along with the vast array of colourful hats and fascinators. It reminded her a little of Ascot Ladies Day, which she'd had the privilege of attending a few times with friends from the Women's Institute. Ascot Ladies Day was as much about the latest fashion, especially in the hat department, as it was about horse racing. It attracted women from all walks of life, including celebrities and royalty. She expected Henley Royal Regatta might be similar, albeit more exclusive in the Stewards' Enclosure.

Moving her eyes on to the men's blazers and suits, Marjorie noticed Frederick grimacing. Horace didn't seem to register his discomfort, continuing his earlier conversation.

"I've booked us a main meal in the Luncheon Tent. It's a la carte. I hope that's all right?"

Spending time with Horace was never boring. He had no problem spending money, but as wealthy as he was, Marjorie and Frederick preferred to pay their way. As for Edna... Well... Edna was Edna.

Having scanned the drinks menu, Marjorie was pleased to see that a variety of teas were available, and she opted for her favourite Earl Grey tea. Frederick and Horace went inside the tent to order, and returned with two lattes, Marjorie's tea and a cup of strong filtered coffee for Edna.

Edna craned her neck towards the river while savouring her coffee. "As interesting as it is checking out the designer clothes, I'd like to see some of these muscular rowers. When do we get to watch anything?"

Marjorie had been wondering the same thing. The daily programme she'd picked up listed many races going on throughout the day, which should have already started, and there were shouts in the distance suggesting something was happening.

"We're close to the finish line, so you'll need to be patient. There's a lot of activity on the far side of the river if you're interested," said Horace.

On the way into the enclosure, they had passed a sign for a water taxi and a long queue. The taxi, Marjorie presumed, transported people to different vantage points along the river. There was also a public enclosure further downriver, which Horace told them was for members of the public who had tickets, and he'd said that locals were aware of free vantage points where they could sneak a glimpse of the races.

One of the large grandstands in their enclosure was filling up. The buzz around the grounds became infectious and a sense of excited anticipation rang through the air. Marjorie sipped her tea, taking it all in.

Her reverie was interrupted when a tall man who looked around the same age as Frederick tapped him on the shoulder. The man's eyes crinkled into a friendly beam.

"Freddy! Is that really you?"

Frederick turned around and beamed back at the man in the maroon blazer. He was white-haired, had dark blue eyes and was sporting a trimmed snow-white beard and moustache. Frederick jumped up. Grabbing the man's hand, he shook it vigorously.

"Jonny, Jonny Sebastian. Well, I never! I didn't expect to meet anyone I knew here, let alone you. It's been years. How are you?"

One thing Marjorie loved about Frederick was the way his grey eyes sparkled when he was happy. Belonging to a timid and somewhat reticent man, his eyes could sometimes be dark and brooding, but when he laughed, they were something else.

"Twenty-two years to be precise, but I'd recognise you and your shirts anywhere."

It was a surprise to discover that Frederick had been wearing his checked shirts for so long. Marjorie had somehow assumed they were an eccentricity that had come with age.

Frederick's face flushed. "What are you doing here, Jonny? I thought you lived in Cornwall."

"I did, still do really, but after Judith died, I had some things to deal with, so I came back to Henley. This is where I grew up."

"For some reason, I thought you hailed from Oxford. Let me introduce you to my friends," said Frederick.

Marjorie was pleased his day was turning out to be better than he had imagined.

"This is Lady Marjorie Snellthorpe."

As Jonny clasped her hand in his, she noticed it was weathered with wrinkled skin, as was his face. "A lady." He winked. "I didn't realise our Freddy moved in such company."

"There's no need for titles. Please call me Marjorie."

"Marjorie it is then."

Frederick continued his introductions, unable to suppress his delight at meeting his old friend. "This is Horace Tyler. He worked in avionics."

The two men shook hands. "Pleased to meet you," said Horace.

"And Edna Parkinton, Marjorie's cousin."

In-law, thought Marjorie, but she said nothing, instead smiling at Frederick's transformation.

"Hello," said Edna.

"This is my good friend Jonny Sebastian. He and I were at university together. We both opened up pharmacies in Bristol until Jonny moved down south."

"We're delighted to meet you," said Marjorie, thinking south was relative as she considered herself a southerner, living in London.

"Won't you join us?" offered Horace.

"Sorry, I can't. Got to work, I'm afraid. I'm a volunteer." He looked at Frederick again. "I miss those Bristol days, Freddy, don't you?"

"Sometimes," said Frederick.

A rotund man with bushy white eyebrows stood a few feet away, glaring at Frederick's old friend. He was next to a woman wearing a pink business suit, and gesturing towards Jonny Sebastian with a polished wooden cane. His voice was loud when he snapped at her.

"What's he doing here?"

"Shush, he'll hear you. Don't be so rude, Jonny's volunteering."

Jonny had indeed heard the man and turned around. The man spun on his heels, marching off in a strop, leaving the smartly dressed woman flashing Jonny an apologetic smile.

"I'd better get back to work, but I finish at five. Would you like to meet at the Bridge Bar and Real Ale Garden for a drink and a catch-up? They do a nice draught."

"I'd love that," said Frederick. "If my friends don't mind?"

"Of course we don't. We can wait for you, Fred. The last race doesn't finish until half past six," said Horace. "Or if you need more time, we can always see you back at the hotel."

"The Stewards' Enclosure closes soon after the last race," said Jonny. "Although they party 'til late on the VIP island. Not your thing, Freddy. I'll see you at five."

As soon as Jonny was out of sight, Edna raised an eyebrow. "*Freddy?* Really, Fred, you should have said."

Poor Frederick was going to be in for endless teasing over the next few days, but he wasn't taking any notice. His face was alight with sheer joy.

THREE

Frederick arrived shortly after five to find the Bridge Bar and Real Ale Garden teeming with people finishing their first day at the regatta with a beer or two. The air was thick with the mingled scent of hops and barley. A variety of strong aftershaves and perfumes occasionally overpowered the aromas being blown towards him by the light breeze.

As he stepped inside the tent, the warmth of bodies packed close together, in stark contrast to the fresher air outside, made him claustrophobic. The low hum of excited chatter permeated throughout the tent, punctuated by occasional bursts of laughter and the clinking of glasses. Frederick caught stronger whiffs of various ales – some crisp and citrusy, others rich and malty.

Being a natural planner, he had scoped the tent and garden out after lunch so that he knew where to come in advance. A busy beer garden wasn't Frederick's idea of fun, but he was partial to real ale, and he was looking forward to catching up with Jonny. Horace had assured Frederick he would enjoy himself and told him to take his time. Frederick was fatigued after driving to Henley the day before and from the early start this morning, but he and his friends had watched a lot of races throughout and he was enjoying the regatta far more than expected, probably because he had bumped into his old friend. The last of the races were continuing when he left the others to meet Jonny.

Edna had fired several jibes his way after the revelation that Jonny called him Freddy. She loved nothing more than shortening people's names, and he and Marjorie put up with being called Fred and Marge, although neither of them liked it. It grated a little that Horace also referred to him as Fred, but Frederick appreciated the fact that Horace had enough respect for Marjorie not to shorten hers. But since Edna had discovered another version of Frederick's name, she was determined to make the most of it. No doubt she would alternate between calling him Fred and Freddy in the future. Jonathan Sebastian was the only person who had ever called him Freddy, and he'd accepted it because Jonathan preferred the name Jonny.

Despite Edna's teasing, Frederick was happy to have run into his old friend, and grateful Edna, Marjorie and Horace had agreed to stay on to watch the last races while he met Jonny for a drink. Frederick hoped Jonny wouldn't want to reminisce late into the night, but was reassured that if he did, they would need to go elsewhere because the enclosure would close its gates not long after the last race. Jonny and Frederick had kept in touch the old-fashioned way, via letter. Now he was keen for the in-person catch-up. It had been far too long, and that was Frederick's fault.

Frederick eyed his friend as he approached the busy bar, but he stopped when he sensed tension. Jonny was engaged in an intense conversation with a man who looked to be around sixty with immaculately groomed dyed black hair. Frederick didn't know whether to interrupt. He forgot his mission momentarily as he observed the scene playing out ahead of him.

"I'm telling you again, Jonny. Nothing untoward happened,

all right? It was a tragedy and you need to let it go. My advice to you is to leave Henley and stop all this nonsense. You're just upsetting people. Why don't you leave the past where it belongs?" Having said his piece, the man turned abruptly, bumping Frederick's shoulder without apologising as he stomped outside.

Jonny turned as if to follow him but put the brakes on when he saw Frederick. "Freddy! I wasn't sure you'd come. Let me buy you a drink. What will you have?"

Jonny's face was ruddier than it had been this morning, and the slurred speech suggested he might already have had a few drinks. *Perhaps he carries a hip flask.* "A pint of the best real ale on offer, please," said Frederick.

"Coming right up." Jonny turned to the bartender and pointed to his glass. "Two of these, Josh. Only the best for my old pal."

The man poured the pints, and Jonny paid.

A woman with spiky blonde hair, dark at the roots, who Frederick hadn't noticed before hissed in Jonny's ear, "Slow down, Jonny. You're not doing yourself any favours."

"It's not me you need to worry about, Sylvia. It's other people. You should know that."

Frederick smiled at the woman named Sylvia, who gave him a brief nod before leaving. She wore a lime green floral dress and as he watched her go, it seemed she knew a lot of people, many of whom stopped her as she headed into the garden.

Moving his eyes away from Sylvia, Frederick asked Jonny, "Who was that man you were speaking to when I arrived?"

"What man?"

"The sleek guy wearing expensive trousers and a maroon blazer like yours."

"Oh him. You forgot to mention the designer watch he never stops looking at."

"I didn't notice that."

"His name's Reginald. He's an old family friend."

"He didn't seem that friendly to me," said Frederick, rubbing his right shoulder which the man had jostled.

"Never mind about him." Jonny handed Frederick his pint, then looked around before setting off through the crowds. Frederick supped the froth from the top of the very full beer glass to prevent it from spilling all over the place. He followed Jonny away from the bar and into the garden. Jonny approached a table a young couple was vacating and placed his glass down before flopping into a chair.

Dappled sunlight reflected off the beer glasses via a large potted fern. Cheers of encouragement reached Frederick's ears from further along the river.

The next race must be underway.

While the two men fell into easy conversation, reminiscing about years gone by and sharing stories of what had happened to their old university pals, many of whom had died, Jonny kept checking over his shoulder or glancing around.

"Is something bothering you, Jonny?" Frederick asked.

His friend smiled, but it didn't reach his eyes. "No. Why should it be?"

"You seem distracted."

"Sorry, Freddy, it's been a long day, that's all. You've moved away from Bristol, if I remember right?"

"Yes, I moved back to Bath. After Flora died, Bristol was never the same. I'd long since sold the shop and I wanted to live somewhere quieter. Bath was familiar, so it seemed as good a place as any. I spend a lot of time travelling these days. If I'm not visiting the kids, I'm staying or holidaying with the friends you met earlier. I'm surprised you moved up here from Cornwall. Are your kids still in St Ives?"

"Funny how we call them kids when they've got kids of their own. But yes, they are. The Henley move is only temporary. I've still got the cottage in Cornwall, but for now, I've moved into my old family home. After my parents died, I rented it out for years to long-term tenants. They recently moved out to buy their own place, so it seemed a good time for me to come back for a bit. I'll be selling the place soon – in fact, Reginald Blackwood, the man you saw me talking to, is touting me for business."

"Oh?"

"He owns a local estate agency" – *that might explain why the man suggested Jonny should move away* – "but I won't sell through him."

Despite him being an old family friend. Something wasn't right here.

"I've still got a few connections in the area. There's something I need to do before I can settle back into life in Cornwall."

"I'm intrigued. Is this something on your bucket list?"

Jonny's eyes darkened to a brooding glare. "Not quite, but maybe it is now you mention it. I might have left it too late now, anyway. It's something I should have done years ago. But I have to try, don't I? If you ever need a place to stay, Freddy, I keep a key under a boulder close to the door."

Jonny wasn't making much sense and, despite his eyes looking as sharp as ever when he wasn't scowling, his speech was becoming more slurred with every gulp of ale. He was smartly dressed, but his white hair was dishevelled.

"I'm not sure you should disclose where you keep house keys in a public place." Frederick turned around to check no-one was listening to their conversation. Jonny tipped his head back, laughing, but it felt forced, and his eyes soon became serious again. "It feels right bumping into you today, Freddy. If I believed in fate, I'd say we were meant to see each other. It's important you should know where the key is. Stash it away in that computer brain of yours. You always were a mine of information."

Frederick wasn't so sure his brain was as quick these days,

but he was grateful for the compliment. "Thanks, Jonny, but there's really no need. We're staying in a beautiful Victorian hotel. Horace – the friend I introduced you to earlier – has many connections..." *Too many*, thought Frederick, but continued, "His granddaughter Dinah has converted a house into a hotel. I can highly recommend her cooking." Frederick would have preferred to be eating rather than drinking right now. The draught beer was tasty but strong, and the alcohol was going to his head. He and his friends had eaten a generous three-course lunch in the Luncheon Tent, but that had been hours ago. "Speaking of food, have you had anything to eat? I'm going to try one of the sausage rolls." Frederick had noticed on the board that sausage rolls were a speciality and sold by the inch.

"No food for me, thanks, but I'll have another pint if you're buying?"

Frederick's glass was still half full whilst Jonny had consumed the contents of his. Jonny never used to be a big drinker, but he had mentioned it being twenty-two years since they had last seen each other and Frederick had to acknowledge people changed with time, especially after losing a spouse.

Once back with a pint of ale for Jonny and a large sausage roll for himself, Frederick consumed a hearty bite before broaching the subject that had been on his mind since they had bumped into each other earlier. "I was sorry not to make it to Judith's funeral after I got your letter about her passing, but I was abroad." Frederick had almost cancelled his planned trip to Romania when he'd received the sad news along with the date of the funeral, but would be eternally grateful he hadn't, otherwise he would never have met the three friends who had transformed his life into something meaningful again. Marjorie, in particular, was the closest friend he had.

"Don't worry about it. I appreciated the letter and the card. She had a good send off. Her dying so suddenly was a shock, though. It's funny. I always thought I'd be the one to go first.

She was as strong as a bear, that one. Then one day" – Jonny clicked his fingers – "gone, just like that."

"It must have been hard."

"It was impossible for a while, but life goes on. Maybe this will be the stuff to kill me." Jonny raised his beer glass.

"You still look as fit as ever to me. On the wife front, I imagined the same thing before Flora died. It's a good thing we never know what the future holds, isn't it?"

Jonny's glazed eyes misted over as they locked onto Frederick's. His index finger tapped his head. "It's the past we need to focus on. That's what moulds us into who we are. We have to put things right." Jonny was rambling again and not really concentrating on Frederick. "You just remember what I said about that key. If you need to get into the place, you've got my permission. Okay?"

His friend's mood was more sombre after the conversation about Judith and the past. Frederick understood and empathised. "Thanks for the offer, but as I said, we're happy where we're staying."

Jonny downed his pint in three goes, becoming less coherent and continuing to look around like a hunted deer.

"Are you expecting someone else?" Frederick asked.

"Nope. What makes you ask?"

"I realise we haven't seen each other in a long time, and forgive me if I'm being presumptuous, Jonny, but I get the impression something's bothering you. You know you can talk to me if you need to?"

Jonny leaned across the table and slapped him on the arm. "You always were too serious, Freddy. Relax and enjoy yourself. There's nothing a few drinks can't cure."

"If you say so," said Frederick, unconvinced. "Tell me about this mission you have up here."

Jonny pushed his empty glass across the table. "It's something I should have done years ago, but I was too busy enjoying myself. And too selfish if I'm honest."

"You never struck me as a selfish man. Is there anything I can do to help?"

"Look, Freddy, it's been great to catch up, but I've got an early start in the morning. I'm going to call it a night. Maybe we can talk again tomorrow when my head's clearer."

"Of course," said Frederick. "Whenever you're ready."

Jonny struggled to his feet, taking a few moments to get his bearings and balance as he wavered. "Now you remember about that key, won't you, Freddy, my boy?"

Frederick felt wretched. What was meant to be a joyful reunion had turned into a depressing encounter. He watched his old friend stagger out of the garden, remembering what he used to be like. Today, Jonny wasn't alone in the drunk department; others a little the worse for wear were vacating the beer garden at the same time.

Cheers erupted from the stands and from both sides of the river, signalling the end of the last race. Frederick got up, leaving the rest of his beer, and headed towards the riverside deckchairs, troubled by his friend's behaviour.

FOUR

The hot and sticky night meant Marjorie tossed and turned until the early hours when she finally gave up and opened a window. The parties and fireworks over the river had ceased to be an issue. Marjorie's mattress was one of those made from memory foam, which provided comfort, but the feather duvet was heavier than she was used to. She made a mental note to ask Dinah for a lighter one. Accustomed to surviving on a few hours' sleep these days, she wasn't concerned by the unsettled night.

Having showered and dressed, Marjorie sat in a chair, gazing through the large central picture window. It had two side windows for opening and had been designed in sympathy to the age of the property, although fitted with double glazing to prevent draughts and traffic noises from disturbing the peace. From her vantage point, there was a clear view of the Thames and St Mary's church tower, which dominated the Henley skyline. The medieval church was one she had found interesting on previous visits to Henley-on-Thames. She wondered about the stories and mysteries the church could reveal and the changes it had witnessed to the place over the centuries.

On hearing a noise below, Marjorie moved her eyes away from the church tower to where she was surprised to see Frederick leaving the hotel and hurrying along the drive. She watched him as he paused to study his phone.

"Silly man's forgotten his hat," Marjorie muttered before quickly sliding her feet into a pair of comfortable shoes and heading downstairs. Removing Frederick's hat from the hook where he'd hung it the night before, she started along the drive after him.

He was only just visible as he turned left out of the gate. Marjorie picked up her pace and followed. Although it was early morning, and Frederick was in no urgent danger from the sun's rays at present, she had noticed his bald head reddening the day before whenever he removed his hat to stop it floating away in the breeze. Marjorie wasn't one for shouting in the street, but needs must.

"Frederick!"

Frederick spun around. "Marjorie! What are you doing?"

"I was going to ask you the same thing. I saw you leaving and noticed you'd forgotten your hat. Where are you off to in such a hurry?"

"I didn't think I'd need the hat, I'm on my way to meet Jonny."

"At this hour?"

"Actually, I'm already late. He must have texted me during the night, but I slept like a log."

"Lucky you," Marjorie mumbled.

"The message said he needed to speak to me urgently before he started his day at the regatta. I was supposed to meet him at five-thirty and it's already six. I'd better be going."

Not ready to give up just yet, Marjorie said, "How extraordinary. Where are you meeting him?"

"That's the hard part. He pinged a location to my phone, but it keeps losing signal and I don't know the area. I've tried messaging him to let him know I'm on my way, but I don't even know if my message sent."

"Show me the location. I might be able to help. I know Henley well."

Marjorie studied the map where the marker was pinpointing the meeting place. "That's Henley Bridge. We passed it yesterday. Would you like me to come with you and show you the way?"

The flustered Frederick sighed with relief. "If you wouldn't mind. I'll get lost otherwise, and I don't want him to think I don't care."

It's hard to get lost in Henley, thought Marjorie, but she said, "Here, put your hat on and follow me. You were going the wrong way, it's not far."

Frederick did as asked and caught up with her in seconds.

"I knew there was something on his mind last night. I tried to ask what it was, but other than admitting he had something to do which he should have done years ago—"

"Yes. I think he mentioned something about that when you asked him why he was in Henley."

"Anyway, he changed the subject on me, denying anything was troubling him. But maybe now he's had time to think about it, he's decided to tell me."

"Did he give you any idea of what the something he had to do might be?"

Frederick shook his head. "Not really. He was drinking heavily. He drank at least two pints while I was with him, probably more before that. And let me tell you, the draught ale they serve at the Bridge Bar is strong. I never finished mine. Edna would say I'm a lightweight."

Marjorie chuckled. "We can't all keep up with Edna."

She pointed to the bridge in the distance and paused. "There it is. Would you like me to leave you now? If your friend has called you out at this early hour, I expect he wants to speak to you in private."

"I guess you'd better—"

Frederick's mouth dropped open, and his eyes widened. Marjorie followed his gaze, staring at the other side of the river where there was an ambulance. Two police cars were parked with blue lights flashing. Marjorie and Frederick hurried onto the bridge, from where they could see a small group of onlookers staring into the water. They peered over the parapet and watched in horror as police waded into the river where a body was tangled in the reeds.

Saying nothing more, Frederick set off at a much brisker pace, almost running in his haste to get to the other side. Marjorie kept up by quickening her stride into what people these days referred to as a power walk. She had recently joined a rambling club and was thankful that their weekend walks had improved her fitness. Although the rambles were not much faster than a stroll, she now rarely needed a cane, although she still carried a fold-up one in her handbag.

When they got close to the scene, Frederick elbowed his way through the small gathering like a crazed man.

"Sorry—Excuse me—Let me through."

Marjorie shadowed him to the front of the onlookers, but Frederick was forced to put his brakes on when a police officer grabbed his arm.

"Where do you think you're going? You can't come through here."

Frederick looked as if he might be about to argue, but instead he peered around the officer. His face crumpled and all colour drained away.

Marjorie's stomach churned over. She recognised the neat white beard and moustache of the man who had been pulled from the water, albeit they were now covered in debris. Frederick's friend Jonny was lying on the ground where paramedics were making a half-hearted attempt to resuscitate him. They wasted little time, not expending much energy when the defibrillator told them what they already knew. The older man and young woman in green ambulance overalls shook their heads.

"He's gone," the man said to a police officer, who nodded. Having confirmed death, the paramedics loaded Jonathan Sebastian onto a stretcher and placed him in the back of the ambulance. The young woman covered him with a blanket and took a seat on the opposite side while the other paramedic slammed the doors closed and climbed into the driver's seat, switching off the flashing blue light.

While the ambulance pulled silently away with no siren, followed by one of the police cars, Frederick stood frozen to the spot, his mouth gaping.

"What happened?" Marjorie asked a rotund woman standing next to her. The woman was struggling to keep hold of the leash as her blue roan cocker spaniel strained at it. The animal did not understand why it was being kept from its walk.

"They found a man in the river. It looks as if he drowned."

"The banks are slippery over this side and the undercurrents can be wicked," added a spindly man with a pinched nose.

"Do you know who found him?" Marjorie asked.

"A group of rowers who were out for a pre-race practice. I heard someone say an oar hit the body tangled in the reeds. They stopped, and a girl screamed. I heard it and arrived soon after. They were just kids and looked really shocked, with no idea what to do. I called the ambulance," said the man. "The emergency services must have sent the police along."

The woman holding tight to the dog's leash took over again. "The police arrived before the ambulance. I expect they were closer and guess they're under pressure to get things cleared up here before the regatta starts again today. That guy over there has been marching up and down demanding they hurry up.

The cops must have known he was dead because they left him in the water for a bit while one of them checked around. The paramedics did their bit after the cops dragged the body out."

Marjorie looked at the man the dog walker pointed out. He was still pacing, using his polished cane like a conductor leading an orchestra through an oratorio. His unmistakable bushy eyebrows and attitude were familiar. It was the same man who had complained about Jonny's presence at the regatta when Marjorie and friends first met him.

"Some people have no respect," the woman continued.

"You can understand it, though," said the spindly man. "You don't want a whole load of police around when the crowds start milling in from all over. An accident like this wouldn't look good for Henley or the regatta."

"How can they be sure it was an accident?" Frederick snapped, emerging from his trance.

"Couldn't be anything else," replied the man. "This lady just told you. The cops looked around before they pulled him out. Besides, this is Henley." As if the latter part of the statement should dismiss any further speculation, the man went on his way, muttering, "Out-of-towners. They've got no idea."

Marjorie was more interested in the agitated man waving his cane around. He was slightly overweight with a ruddy complexion and wore a similar blazer to Horace's, along with a regatta tie. His shoes were dirty and the bottom third of his trousers were wet, both out of keeping with the rest of his attire. This time, he gestured at the small crowd with his immaculately polished cane which never touched the ground.

"Get them out of here," he demanded. "And that squad car."

Another officer joined the one who had been barring the onlookers' way, and they moved towards their vehicle parked on a grass verge. The regatta man tutted before calling out, "Show's over. You're free to be on your way."

Frederick ignored him, marching over to the officer getting into the second car. "Is that it?"

The woman's forehead wrinkled. "Pardon?"

"Aren't you going to investigate?"

"Investigate what, sir?"

Frederick sucked his lips in, his voice shaking, but rising a few decibels as he spoke. "A man has just been fished out of the river. I would have thought the least you could do is to consider whether foul play is involved. Where's the forensic team?"

"Thank you for pointing out what we should do, sir, but the evidence suggests a man fell into the river and drowned."

The other officer leaned on the roof of the driver's side, frowning. "There's no reason to suspect otherwise, mate. This is Henley." He climbed inside the car.

That phrase again. Marjorie intervened. "My friend knew the dead man. They had arranged to meet this morning."

The officer nearest to them softened. "I'm sorry for your loss, sir. Could I take your name in case we need to speak to you?"

Frederick gave his name and telephone number. "We're staying at Dinah's Hotel."

"Where are they taking Mr Sebastian? And would you like Frederick to identify the body?" Marjorie asked.

"He'll go to the Oxford Radcliffe Infirmary mortuary, and there's no need for that. Sir Andrew has already given us preliminary information about the deceased. When we've tracked down his family, they will be visited by the local force in Cornwall."

"If you need a contact for them, I may have it in my address book," said Frederick.

"No need. We're known for our efficiency, sir."

"Come on, Trish." The officer inside the car was becoming impatient.

"If there's nothing else?"

"I... I... don't suppose so," said Frederick.

The officer named Trish climbed into the car and it skidded away, leaving Frederick and Marjorie staring after it in astonishment. The man with the bushy eyebrows, who they assumed to be Sir Andrew, had now left the scene and the small crowd had mostly dispersed, continuing their day as if a body in the water was an everyday occurrence, even if it was Henley!

Marjorie approached the lady with the spaniel again.

"Do you know the surname of that man, Sir Andrew?"

"Is that the bossy guy? No, sorry. I don't know any sirs."

"Did you see if he helped pull the body from the water?"

"No. He turned up after the police got here and just started shouting orders."

"Thank you."

It wouldn't be that difficult to find out who Sir Andrew was, although Marjorie suspected it might be exactly what it looked like: an accidental death.

A flock of geese honked as they flew overhead, announcing their arrival. She looked up at the traditional V formation and watched the birds land on the water to take up their space. No doubt they would be in a hurry to have a good feed before the day's racing began. Henley Bridge wasn't too far from the finishing line. If she and Frederick hadn't been present ten minutes ago, no-one other than those who witnessed it would be wise to the fact that a body had been recovered from the river.

Will the local press be kept informed about what has occurred? Perhaps, as most reporters worth their salary will find out anyway and decide whether it merits a few lines or further investigation. Without evidence of foul play, they would be more than likely to fill the local front pages with famous faces attending the regatta. Edna had pointed out a few reality television celebrities and lifestyle gurus Marjorie had never heard of the evening before.

Frederick remained fixed to the spot, staring at the area

where the ambulance crew had tried to resuscitate his old friend. Marjorie took his arm. "I'm so sorry about Jonny, Frederick, but I don't think there's any more we can do here."

When he forced his eyes to look at her, they were misted over. The two of them began the walk back to the hotel in silence.

FIVE

Frederick struggled to move his legs. They felt like lead as he and Marjorie took the road back to the hotel. The cheerful bustle of Henley-on-Thames, with its quaint shops and excited regatta-goers, seemed a world away from the grim scene he'd just witnessed. He registered the concerned glance Marjorie threw his way, but he was lost in a fog of disbelief and memory.

"It's hard to believe he's gone," he murmured, more to himself than to Marjorie. "We meet up after all these years and then this... I should have pushed him on what was bothering him last night."

"I'm so sorry, Frederick, but you tried. You said he'd been drinking," Marjorie said softly.

He felt her comforting hand on his arm. The simple gesture threatened to unravel Frederick's composure. He blinked rapidly, fighting back the sting of tears. It was the shock as much as anything, and the realisation that he might have been able to do something.

As they ambled through the streets of Henley, his memory became blurred and shifted to the halls of Bristol University where he'd first met Jonny all those years ago. He remembered it vividly – the first day, both of them had got lost in the labyrinthine corridors and were going to be late for the same lecture. They'd literally collided outside the lecture hall, Frederick sending Jonny's books and papers flying. He'd been so nervous but Jonny had laughed: a warm, infectious chortle that had immediately put Frederick at ease.

"Well," Jonny had said, as Frederick helped him pick up his scattered belongings, "I suppose we can't make much of a worse first impression than this, can we? I'm Jonny, Jonny Sebastian."

"Frederick Mackworth. Are you studying pharmacology?"

"Indeed, I am. You?"

"The same."

From that moment on, they'd been inseparable. Frederick had never found it easy to make friends and had feared spending countless nights alone at university. But late-night study sessions fuelled by cheap coffee and shared dreams had become a part of their routine. Jonny was always the outgoing one, drawing Frederick out of his shell and into new experiences. Frederick, in turn, provided a steady grounding influence for his more impulsive friend.

"When we were at university, Jonny was always larger than life," Frederick said, his voice thick with emotion. "He had a way of making everything we did an adventure."

Marjorie squeezed his arm gently, encouraging him to continue.

"I remember this one time," Frederick went on, a hint of a smile playing at his lips, "we were revising for our finals. Jonny burst into my room at midnight, insisting we needed a break. Next thing I knew, we were climbing to the top of the tower of Wills Memorial Building – strictly forbidden, of course. I was always more daring when I was with him. We sat up there until dawn, talking about our hopes for the future, watching the city wake up below us. For that one night, it felt like we could conquer the world."

The smile faded as quickly as it had appeared. "And we did in our own way. We both opened pharmacies, married wonderful people and life was perfect for a while. I missed him when he moved to Cornwall but he always had a restless spirit. I should have kept in touch more after his wife died. Life just... got in the way, I suppose."

They walked in silence for another few minutes, the weight of what they had witnessed by the river hanging heavy in the air.

"At least you kept in touch. Many people don't and often regret it."

"You know," Frederick continued, his brow furrowed, "Jonny wasn't always easy to be friends with. He could be moody and unpredictable, sometimes he'd shout and throw things around for no obvious reason. It was that side of him I saw again last night. Sometimes he'd disappear for days, then show up as if nothing had happened. But he was also the most loyal friend you could ask for. Whenever I needed him, he'd drop everything in a heartbeat."

"We each have our inner demons," said Marjorie. "We do our best to conquer them and live a life that's worth something."

Frederick considered what Marjorie said. She was right, of course.

As they neared the hotel, Frederick's pace slowed. He wasn't ready to face the others yet, to answer their well-meaning questions or endure pitying looks.

"Jonny had changed over the years but I didn't want to see it," he said quietly. "In his letters, I mean. He seemed... I don't know, more restless, maybe. Like he was searching for something, particularly after Judith died. It was obviously this mission he mentioned that was on his mind. I wish I'd pressed him more about it when we met yesterday. It's just I'm not the pushy kind. I should have..."

His voice trailed off, choked with regret.

Marjorie stopped walking, turning to face Frederick. Her bright blue eyes locked onto his. "You couldn't have known what was going to happen, Frederick. You had gone your separate ways as we all do. And now, the best thing you can do for Jonny is to remember the good times, and the close friendship you had."

Frederick nodded, taking a deep breath.

As they resumed their walk, he felt a sort of resolve forming. Jonny had always encouraged him to step out of his comfort zone, to take risks. Now, it was time for Frederick to honour his friend's memory by doing just that.

"You're right, Marjorie," he said, his voice steadier. "The least I can do for him is to find out what happened. And that might mean doing things I don't want to do. But if the tables were turned, I know he would have done the same for me." He wondered whether that was true. Jonny's letters had become more infrequent with the passage of time. If Frederick hadn't written regularly, would his friend have stopped writing? Now, he'd never know, but for the times Jonny had protected Frederick from bullies at university, he would do what had to be done.

With a grim determination, he entered the hotel with Marjorie by his side.

SIX

"There you are, Marge. I might have known you two would be skulking out early in the morning for a romantic stroll."

Edna's straight talking had lost most of its shock value over time, but there were occasions when it still jarred. "We were not skulking anywhere" – *and it was far from romantic* – "we merely went for a walk."

"Well, hurry and get your breakfast order in before any of the later guests turn up. Horace is having scrambled eggs and I've ordered a full English."

Recalling the scene she and Frederick had so recently witnessed, Marjorie felt her stomach lurch at the image of a fried breakfast. The mere smell of bacon coming from the kitchen made her feel nauseous but, inhaling through her mouth and giving Frederick's arm a gentle pat, she accompanied him and Edna into the dining room.

Horace was leafing through a morning paper. He looked up smiling and folded the newspaper away.

"Good morning. Did you sleep well?"

"As well as can be expected, thank you," said Marjorie. "It was rather muggy."

"Well, I had a wonderful night's sleep," said Edna, dropping herself into a chair and taking a slice of fresh toast from the rack. She slathered it with butter and marmalade.

"It must have been all that champagne," said Horace, wiggling his eyebrows in jest.

Dinah, Horace's granddaughter, emerged from the kitchen carrying a large pot of tea. "I heard you come in, Lady Marjorie. Good morning, Mr Mackworth," she added.

Frederick didn't reply but forced a nod.

"Thank you, Dinah," said Marjorie. "Tea is just what I need."

"What can I get you for breakfast this morning?"

"I'd love a bowl of grapefruit please, that and a slice of toast will be ample for me. We ate rather late last night."

"And for you, Mr Mackworth?"

"Call him Fred. I do," said Edna.

"He prefers Frederick," said Marjorie, giving Edna a glare.

"I'm not hungry. Could I just have a pot of strong coffee please?"

"Of course." Dinah frowned but returned to the kitchen.

Unlike Edna, Horace showed concern. "Are you ill, Fred? You look a bit out of sorts."

"I'm fine," muttered Frederick.

"Oh great, he's going to be in one of his moods again," said Edna, tutting. "I hope you snap out of it because I can't be doing with looking at your long face all day."

On occasions, Edna's insensitiveness was almost too much to bear. Frederick didn't respond, which was worrying because he could usually offer some form of defence when Edna goaded him. Instead, he looked down at his trembling hands.

Dinah broke the silence, bringing through a pot of coffee for Frederick and a bowl of grapefruit for Marjorie while her assistant placed Edna's enormous breakfast on the table. Dinah returned to the kitchen, coming back a moment later with Horace's scrambled eggs. Horace began munching.

Once the dining room was empty, Marjorie could hear Dinah and her assistant chatting from the kitchen about a shopping list. Marjorie glanced back through the open dining-room door into the hallway to check none of the other guests were about to arrive before saying anything.

"Frederick's had a shock this morning. To be honest, we both have."

Horace and Edna ate and listened while Marjorie related the events that had occurred since they left the house first thing. Frederick sipped coffee, but barely said a word. His grey eyes remained dull.

After hearing the story, Edna stopped chomping through bacon for a moment and cast a sheepish look at Frederick. "Sorry, Fred, I didn't realise. You should have said something when you came in."

He didn't get the opportunity, thought Marjorie.

"I'm still in shock," said Frederick.

"Poor man. It can't have been easy for you, seeing him like that," said Edna.

"We weren't too close to the body, but it wasn't pleasant," said Marjorie.

"Why did he text you in the middle of the night in the first place? What did he want to talk to you about so urgently?" Horace asked.

Frederick shrugged. "I don't know. When we had a drink last night, he told me he'd come back to Henley to sort something out. Something that should have been done years ago, he said. He wouldn't elaborate – he'd had too much to drink, to be honest. When I arrived at the Bridge Bar, he was arguing with someone. I heard the guy telling Jonny he should let something go and leave Henley. Now he's dead. It feels off to me. I need to find out what it was Jonny came back to Henley to do."

"Maybe he got sick of tourists in Cornwall and wanted a break," said Edna. "There doesn't have to be anything more to it than that."

"Then why would he say what he did?"

"I don't know. Some people like to appear mysterious to make themselves more interesting than they are."

Frederick shook his head. "No. Jonny implied he'd sell his parents' home and move back to Cornwall once he'd done what he had come to do. That reminds me, he told me the guy he argued with was an estate agent named Reginald, although he denied they were arguing at all."

"Maybe it was friendly banter," said Edna.

"Selling the house might explain why this Reginald was trying to get Jonny to leave Henley," said Marjorie.

"There was more to it than that."

"But even if your friend had some mission, it could have been anything. Perhaps it was to do with the legal stuff. Maybe there were other people entitled to part of the estate."

"No. He was an only child and had been renting the house out for years."

"Well, it's hard to imagine you'll find out what it was now he's fallen into the river," said Horace.

"I don't believe he fell into the river. And even if he did, he wouldn't have drowned. Jonny was an excellent swimmer."

Horace's eyebrows knitted together, but Edna was dismissive.

"The same could be said of all of us at one time. We're not what we once were. In case you haven't noticed, we're a lot older now, aren't we?"

"That may be. I was never any good at swimming, could barely keep my head above the water, but Jonny regularly swam. And he went wild swimming most days."

"I thought you hadn't seen the guy in twenty-odd years," said Edna.

Marjorie had to inwardly admit to thinking the same thing.

"We kept in touch. In his letters, Jonny always mentioned swimming and water sports. He used to tease me about taking me wild swimming one day, knowing I didn't like being in the water. He loved it. Swimming was his hobby during his working life and his passion after he retired."

Marjorie rubbed her temple. "When was the last time you wrote to each other? You seemed surprised he was living in Henley."

"It was when his wife died. The summer we all met in Romania. I didn't go to the funeral and felt guilty about it. I wrote a few times, but he hadn't been in touch for a while. Last night I apologised for not attending the funeral and he told me it was okay, which was a weight off my mind."

"He could have stopped swimming after the bereavement," said Horace. "We can't be certain he was still a strong swimmer, or if he swam in the Thames after moving to Henley."

"No, we can't," Frederick admitted. "But apart from having too much to drink, he looked fit and healthy to me."

"River currents can be deadly. The man we spoke to earlier said as much," said Marjorie. "But if you think the issue bothering your friend might have led to his death, Frederick, I'm willing to trust your instincts."

"Thank you. That means a lot. I just can't get my head around it. I can't believe he drowned."

Edna's eyes almost popped out of her head as she slapped it with her palm. "Here we go again! You can't seriously think someone knocked the guy off because he was a bit out of sorts. Perhaps seeing you sparked memories of happier times. Youthful reminiscences. Maybe, just maybe, he came to Henley to kill himself and that's why he wouldn't talk about it."

Frederick's head shot up. "Why would you think that?"

"I'm sorry for your loss, Fred, I really am, but people

change, and perhaps he was meeting you this morning to tell you his last wishes and all that."

"I hate to admit it, but Edna's got a valid point," said Horace. "Better to tell an old friend, if that's what he was about to do, than his immediate family."

Frederick's hands trembled as he put his cup back on its saucer. "And I was late. If that was his intention, I should have been there, and maybe I could have talked some sense into him."

"Hang on a minute," said Marjorie. "There is no evidence that Frederick's friend committed suicide."

"And presumably nothing that made the police think it was a suspicious death either," countered Edna.

Marjorie had been considering the police response and the presence of the bombastic Sir Andrew. "I believe the police were steamrollered into coming to a quick conclusion," she said.

"What makes you say that?" Horace asked, polishing off the last of his scrambled egg and refilling his coffee cup.

Marjorie poured herself a second cup of tea when Dinah appeared to clear the table. "Are you sure you won't eat anything?" she asked Frederick.

"Perhaps I'll have some toast," he said.

As Edna had just taken the last slice, Dinah took the empty rack. "I'll fill this up and be right back."

Once Dinah had returned with a fresh rack of toast, another pot of coffee and one of tea, and refilled the milk jug, Marjorie answered Horace's question.

"There was a rather pompous man bossing everyone about. A bystander commented on it, too. This Sir Andrew, one of the police officers referred to him as, more or less identified the body and sent them packing. The interesting thing is that I noticed him gesturing angrily towards Jonny at the regatta yesterday. He made it clear he was annoyed by Jonny's presence. I would say Sir Andrew is a man of influence."

"That may be, but I can understand him not wanting an unexpected death interrupting proceedings with the regatta taking place. I'm sure the police would have done their due diligence before allowing the body to be moved," said Horace.

"They say they did. It just seems a coincidence that a man who appeared to dislike Frederick's friend would be in the place where his body was found, let alone actively pushing the police to reach a swift conclusion."

"Sir Andrew, did you say?" Horace was stroking his chin, eyes scrunched.

"Yes. Do you know him?"

"It rings a bell. Let me think about it."

"What else did Jonny tell you last night, Frederick? Did he say anything more about the man Reginald, the one he supposedly didn't argue with?" Marjorie asked.

Frederick shook his head while chewing on a slice of toast. "Not really. He skimmed over the matter and told me Reginald was an old family friend, but he wasn't behaving like one. It wasn't that Sir Andrew, though. When he mentioned the guy owned an estate agent's and was touting for business, he said he would never sell through him."

"I can't believe what I'm hearing!" said Edna. "Why won't you lot just have a nice jolly without being determined to turn a tragic accident into a murder?"

"Wasn't it you who summoned us all to Harrogate a few months ago to do the same thing?" Horace said gently.

"And your instincts were right, Edna. Frederick trusted you; I think it's only fair that you trust him about this," Marjorie added.

Edna pouted, but sighed. "I suppose if you put it like that. But what do you want to do about it? There's not a lot to go on."

"It's clear the police will not investigate unless anything suspicious crops up during the post-mortem," said Marjorie.

"We could speak to this Reginald fellow and see if he'll tell us what Jonny was doing that he objected to."

"That's a good place to start," said Horace, looking at his watch. "Now, I think we should leave. We've already missed the first race."

Edna puffed her cheeks, blowing out the air through pursed lips. "Maybe this investigation will be more interesting than a bunch of posh people rowing up and down the river."

Horace snorted a laugh. "Stop pretending, Edna. You enjoyed yourself yesterday, and if I remember rightly, you won a fair bit of money."

"I didn't know you were betting on the races," said Marjorie.

Edna tapped her nose. "Just goes to show you're not as good a sleuth as you think you are."

Horace got up and popped his head around the kitchen door. "Thank you, Dinah. We might be late in again this evening."

"No problem, Granddad. I can leave sandwiches out if you like."

"Don't go to any trouble. There's plenty of food at the regatta and if we're hungry, we'll get a meal at the pub like we did last night."

Edna opened her mouth to complain but Marjorie took her elbow. "I can assure you; you won't starve. Now come along, we've got work to do."

"I'm not sure why I'm agreeing to this."

"Out of the kindness of your heart," said Horace, bringing up the rear. "And to help a friend," he whispered.

"If it turns out to be a false alarm, *Freddy's* going to owe me big time," said Edna.

And I'm sure he will never hear the end of it, thought Marjorie. Somehow, though, she suspected Frederick's suspicions were well founded and likely to be proven correct. If they could discover what it was Jonny Sebastian had returned to Henley to do, they might find out whether it had cost him his life. If only he'd shared his mission with Frederick. For now, all they had was the fact that two men didn't appear happy to have Jonny at the regatta, with one telling him to leave Henley altogether. Could it be something to do with the regatta itself?

She hoped for Frederick's sake that Jonny hadn't taken his own life because he would take it badly and blame himself. However the tragedy unfolded, the three of them would support him. Even Edna would help where she could, although Marjorie couldn't guarantee her cousin-in-law wouldn't complain about it.

SEVEN

After queuing for around fifteen minutes, Marjorie and her three friends entered the Stewards' Enclosure, as they had done on the previous day. Thankfully, Henley Bridge wasn't visible and they hadn't had to pass the place where Frederick's friend had been found. Frederick had barely said a word on the way.

The rowing was already in full swing with rival clubs on the water when they arrived. People cheered with gusto and it was hard not to get wrapped up in the atmosphere. Edna hurried them towards the Coffee and Ices tent and Horace got the drinks, although Marjorie insisted on paying.

It wasn't long before the caffeine did its job. Frederick lifted his head, his eyes eager.

"Let's try to find this Sir Andrew whatever his name is and quiz him about what happened."

"Or we could watch the racing," Edna retorted, with her usual eye roll.

"Edna! You promised to help," said Marjorie. "Besides, I thought you weren't keen on watching posh people racing along the river."

"Sarcasm doesn't suit you, Marge. But don't worry, I'll help.

I'll ask at the bar if they know who this bloke is." Before anyone had a chance to stop her, Edna was barging past people in the drinks queue and interrogating a young man whose face turned bright red while he was under the cosh from the force in front of him. His eyes showed incredulity.

"You'd better rescue that young man before she frightens him to death," Marjorie said to Horace.

"Not to mention rescuing Edna from the ire of the people in the queue waiting to be served," said Frederick, forcing a smile.

Horace was quick to his feet and dissuaded Edna from terrorising the poor worker any further. A few people in the queue nodded to Horace in gratitude as he encouraged her back to their table.

"He didn't know anything," said Edna, pouting. "Young people these days don't notice the world around them. Too busy on their phones if you ask me."

"Or trying to serve customers," said Marjorie with a smile.

"You asked me to help and I'm helping," said Edna taking a gulp of iced tea.

Not the kind of help I had in mind, thought Marjorie, resisting the urge to point out that getting thrown out of the enclosure for harassment wouldn't benefit their cause. The truth was that Edna's unconventional approach sometimes uncovered information from unlikely sources. Marjorie just wished she didn't go about it like a bull charging a matador.

Horace nudged Frederick. "You're good on the internet, Fred. Why don't you try a search?"

Frederick perked up, retrieving his phone from his inside jacket pocket. Moments later, after a few taps of the screen, he said. "Found him! Sir Andrew Eccles was knighted for his contribution to rowing. He used to be an amateur rower at a club in Norfolk and worked to get local schools involved. He lives in a place called Filby and has a boating business on the Norfolk Broads. It says here, he's a donor and keen follower of the Henley Royal Regatta and has attended every year for the past thirty-five years."

The cheering around them got louder as the next race neared the finishing line. Edna stood up, trying to see who was in the lead.

"I hope that was my team," she said.

"Don't tell me you've put another bet on?" said Horace.

"You're the one to blame, Horace Tyler. If you hadn't given me tips about who you thought would win—"

"As interesting as your gambling habits might be, Edna, do you mind if we get back to the matter in hand?" Marjorie said.

"It's only a little flutter and so much for this being on your bucket list, Marge. If you miss all the races, don't think I'm coming back again next year."

Edna had a point. Marjorie had looked forward to being at the regatta ever since Horace had booked it, but she also had to help Frederick. She could console herself with taking in the atmosphere for now.

"Sir Andrew Eccles would have to be a significant donor to wield the influence we observed this morning," she said, thoughtfully.

"Or just loud," said Edna.

Pot and kettle came to mind. Biting her tongue, Marjorie donned her reading glasses to examine the information on Frederick's phone screen.

"He's seventy-seven. I wonder how he knew Jonny," said Frederick. "He doesn't hail from Henley and I don't remember seeing him at university."

Horace slapped himself on the head. "I *do* remember him. Our paths crossed a few times over business. Can't say I took to him: a womaniser and a bighead."

Edna burst out laughing. "Your twin then?"

Horace grinned. "Does he have anything to do with boating in Cornwall?" he asked.

"Not that I can find on this Wiki page. I'll check his social media trail later, but for now, let's do as Edna suggests and enjoy a few races. I don't want to ruin your holiday chasing shadows. The more I think about it, the more I'm coming to the conclusion that Jonny's death was an accident."

Or suicide, thought Marjorie but refrained from suggesting it.

With the decision made, the four headed for their reserved deckchairs. The weather, though hotting up, couldn't have been better. A satisfying breeze from the Thames made for comfortable viewing and the air was less humid. Marjorie kept a close eye on Frederick, concerned he might be eager to investigate his friend's death and that he was watching the racing for her benefit against his better judgement. She needn't have worried. Frederick's eyes watched eagerly as three boats whizzed into view, accompanied by cheers.

The rowers' faces were strained as they stretched every sinew of the muscles in their arms, each focused on the task in hand. The oars hit the water in complete synchronicity while the boats gleamed in the sunlight. Two were battling it out for the lead while one struggled to keep up. Yet others were a full boat length behind. Commentary bellowed through the loudspeaker, urging the rowers on as the cheers got louder and louder.

"What race is this?" Edna shouted to be heard above the noise. "They look like a bunch of old codgers."

"Hardly! It's the over-fifties race, Edna – go on, boys!" said Horace, excited. "I could have had a go at this one myself."

"Not without a defibrillator at hand." Edna chortled, setting off one of their joint snorting sessions. Even Marjorie chuckled at the thought of Horace trying to keep pace with the group of six men who were straining to hold the lead.

"That would be us back there," Horace said, pointing to a boat trailing right at the rear, rowed by a much older group.

"Wrinkly snails we could be called," shouted Edna as the roars got even louder. Marjorie thought her ears would burst.

But Frederick wasn't listening... or cheering. His eyes were transfixed on the two boats battling it out for the win. They were being carried to the finishing line by people in the grandstand behind who were on their feet.

"They're fast, aren't they?" cried Marjorie, trying to get Frederick's attention.

"It's him," yelled Frederick, getting up and raising binoculars to his eyes.

"Who?"

"Reginald. The guy who was warning Jonny off last night. I need to speak to him."

Frederick was out of his chair and hurrying towards the place where the boats came ashore. Marjorie nudged Horace.

"Come on. Frederick's spotted the estate agent from last night."

Edna huffed at the interruption but followed, anyway.

They had to wait a while for the noise to die down and for the exhausted rowers to come ashore. The winners struggled out of their boat and had to support each other to stand for photographs. Well-wishers eventually moved on, and Frederick ambled over. He went straight for a lean man with smooth black hair and a wide grin on his face.

"Thanks for stepping in, Reginald, we couldn't have done it without you," said one of the six, slapping the man on the back while opening a bottle of champagne.

"Glad to help."

"Excuse me?" Frederick tapped him on the shoulder. "Do you mind if I ask you something?"

"Sure. But I haven't got a lot of time," said Reginald.

"I noticed you speaking to an old friend of mine last night at the Bridge Bar."

Reginald's jaw tensed. "I spoke to many people last night."

"Jonathan Sebastian was his name, otherwise known as Jonny. You might have heard he died this morning."

Frederick wasn't usually this forthright, but it was having the desired effect. "I heard. That's the reason I raced today."

"Are you saying Jonathan Sebastian was supposed to race?" Marjorie asked. "Wasn't he, erm... too old?" She couldn't believe she was saying this having herself gone snorkelling not so long ago.

Another man stepped forward, giving Reginald a congratulatory pat on the back. "Good race." He turned to Marjorie. "We're not ageist here – as long as a man or woman passes their physical, they can race. Jonny was fit enough. I often saw him wild swimming when I took my boat out on the Thames" – Frederick shot a 'told you so' look at Edna – "We were all sad to hear about his drowning."

"It sounds as though you knew him well," Marjorie remarked.

"A long time ago. I grew up in Henley and his family did too. But he moved away, and we only met up again recently."

"Oswald Greene's a veteran coach, he advised us how to win," said Reginald.

Ignoring Oswald, Frederick focussed on Reginald. "I wanted to ask what you and Jonny were arguing about last night?"

"Arguing? Who said we were arguing?"

"I do. I saw you."

Reginald was now scowling and making ready to turn his back on them until Horace held out his hand. "Congratulations on the race. I used to row a bit myself, the way you worked together impressed me."

Reginald relaxed. "Thank you, I see you're a member." He eyed Horace's badge. "Considering it was a last-minute switch, we did all right."

"Horace. Horace Tyler, pleased to meet you."

Reginald took the hand that was waiting to be shaken. "Reginald Blackwood."

"This is Edna, she's more pleased than the rest of us you won. She put a bet on you."

Reginald grinned. "The drinks are on you then."

"And this is Lady Marjorie Snellthorpe and Fred Mackworth, but you've already met them. Fred's upset about the death of his old university pal. We were wondering whether you thought he had anything on his mind when you spoke to him last night?"

Being part of the old school-tie club, as Edna would call it, certainly helped Horace with speaking to privileged men like Reginald. The ice melted.

"I wish I could help. Jonny hadn't been back in Henley long, but the team was glad to welcome him. He was a good rower. I don't row competitively these days." There was a tinge of bitterness in the younger man's voice.

"Jonny told Frederick he had come back to Henley to do something important. Do you have any idea what that might have been?" Marjorie asked.

Reginald shrugged. "To take part in the race most likely, and he planned to sell his family home. I expect you know his parents died a while ago?"

"Jonny enjoyed rowing when I knew him so I expect that was it," added Oswald. "Anyway, Reginald, we'd better get this boat moved and have a celebration drink."

"Thanks for your time. And again, great race," said Horace.

As the four friends turned to go, another man came after them, catching up with Frederick. "I got to know Jonny a bit, but people say he wasn't the same man they remembered since he got back. From my chats with him, he never got over Michael. That's what he was doing here. Looking for answers, then he planned to return to Cornwall."

"Who's Michael?" Frederick asked.

"I didn't know him, he died about twenty years ago. Michael was Jonny's cousin. He drowned close to where they found Jonny this morning. That's all I know. It wouldn't surprise me if Jonny took his own life. He missed his wife terribly and I don't think he was getting very far in his search for answers. How could he? These tragedies happen."

Oswald Greene was glaring in their direction.

"Look, I'd better go. Sorry for your loss," he said to Frederick.

Frederick's shoulders slumped. "If only I'd got that text message sooner."

"We still don't know for certain what happened," said Marjorie.

"I agree," said Horace. "And that Reginald chap knew more than he was letting on. Why was he so cagey?"

"Yeah, I didn't like our designer man, Reggie at all. Definitely hiding something. Fred, I hate to admit it, but your friend might not have died by accident."

"Quite, Edna," said Marjorie. "I suggest we find out more about Jonny's cousin Michael, and about Reginald Blackwood."

"What about that coach fella? Smarmy so and so," said Edna. "And why did you say I had a bet on their race, Horace? I didn't even know it was on."

"It seemed a good idea and it cut through the tension. They were getting all defensive with our Fred here being so blunt. I didn't know you had it in you," he said, slapping Frederick on the arm.

"What now, then?" asked Edna.

Frederick stopped dead. "The key!" he shouted, tapping his forehead with his finger.

Marjorie stared at him. "What key?"

"Last night, Jonny kept going on and on about a key to his house. He told me where he put it and insisted I remember. He said that if I needed to get inside, I had his permission. I thought he was rambling."

"But now you think his mentioning the key was significant," Marjorie said.

"It's as if he had a premonition that something might happen to him and he wanted me to know how to get into his place if it did."

"Or he knew he was going to kill himself and that's where he's left the note," said Edna.

"Right. Next stop, Jonny's house," said Horace.

"I don't know his Henley address," said Frederick.

"You mean after all his hullabaloo about making sure you knew where his key was, you didn't ask where he lived?"

"He wasn't to know, Edna. I suggest we have an early lunch and see if we can find an address. Can that be arranged, Horace?"

"I'll make a call," he said.

"How will we find his address?" Edna crossed her arms.

"I have access to a family tree website," said Marjorie. "If we have either of his parents' first names, Horace or Frederick could log into my account and find the address."

"His father's name was Jonathan," said Frederick. "That's why he liked the name Jonny because people got them mixed up when he was a child and he didn't like being called junior."

Edna took Marjorie's arm. "Did I ever tell you, you're smarter than you look, Marge?"

EIGHT

It was a lot easier to track down Jonny's parents' address than Marjorie had imagined. A taxi dropped them off on the Oxfordshire side of the river. They were on a road lined with a row of gorgeous Victorian properties.

"Imagine the stories these could tell," said Horace.

Marjorie often wondered the same thing when she came across old properties. She knew the history of her own home in Hampstead Heath because she had researched it thoroughly.

Marjorie was dragged from her musings as they meandered along the wide pavement by Frederick turning right and marching along the driveway of the address they were seeking. "He said the key was under a boulder next to the door."

Marjorie, Horace and Edna followed Frederick through the open wrought-iron gates, which couldn't have been closed for many years as overgrown weeds blocked them. The wide pebbled driveway was also in a state of disrepair.

"Doesn't look like the place has been maintained," remarked Horace.

They arrived at a front storm porch where climbing roses formed a natural arch. These had at least been clipped back to allow room for people to enter. There were no boulders in sight, just two old and moss-covered concrete statues of Great Danes on either side of the porch. Once upon a time they would have provided an impressive first greeting but those days were long gone.

Horace took the lead, heaving one and then the other while Frederick checked underneath. Nothing but woodlice and crumbling concrete.

"These haven't been moved in years, Fred."

"Perhaps the boulder is by the back door," said Marjorie. "From a safety point of view, it would make more sense."

"Leaving keys in the open anywhere makes no sense to me," said Edna. "Not in this day and age."

"This is Henley!" Frederick and Marjorie blurted out in unison, before laughing.

Edna frowned. "What's so funny?"

"Sorry, Edna. When Frederick raised doubts about his friend's death being an accident early this morning, two people used the phrase, 'This is Henley'. It was as if it explained everything."

Horace chuckled. "I'm sure there is a low crime rate in Henley-on-Thames compared to the bigger places not too far away. People don't like to imagine their own sleepy town being polluted by the suggestion of foul play."

Frederick wiped his hands with a handkerchief, having been feeling around under the statues. "I'd hardly call Henley sleepy at the moment. It's heaving."

"The regatta certainly puts it on the map, along with other high-profile events," Horace conceded, looking over his shoulder as he wandered around to the side of the house. "I expect it's a mixed blessing for the residents. On the one hand it improves the local economy and on the other, it disrupts their lives."

"The taxi driver said traffic comes to a standstill unless you know the side roads," said Marjorie.

Two more wrought-iron gates barred the entrance to the rear of the property. This time they were closed and around eight foot high. A padlock and chain held them together.

"Now what?" The words were only just out of Edna's mouth when they watched in astonishment as Horace clambered over the gate. A man in his eighties wearing his best clothes and performing gymnastics to get to the other side had a comical edge.

"Don't snag your posh blazer," called Edna.

"Never mind that. Let's hope there's no CCTV," he said, puffing after dropping to the other side. He doubled over, catching his breath before moving. "I hope the key's here because I'm not sure I could do that again. Wait there a minute." Horace disappeared and was soon back again holding a key in his hand. "Got it. Go to the front door and I'll let you in."

"Let's hope there isn't a Rottweiler in there," said Marjorie, recalling the huge dog called Hercules that had arrived with her temporary cook the Christmas before last.

"You don't think there is, do you?" Edna, for all her blather, was fond of Horace.

"Not at all. I'm sure Jonny wouldn't have told Frederick about the key if there was a guard dog."

The three of them hurried back to the front door, pleased that trees shielded the driveway, keeping them hidden from view. A bright red sports car was parked in front of the attached garage.

"Do you think that belonged to Jonny?"

"He liked fast cars," replied Frederick.

Moments later they heard a latch turning from inside, and Horace pulled open the heavy solid oak door. Dirt and debris covered the stained-glass side windows preventing light from entering the hallway.

"Sorry it took a while. The backdoor key is rusty and the lock stiff. I don't think the key was used that often. There's a cleaner one hanging on a hook inside," he said. "Be warned, Fred. Your friend left the place in a mess."

Frederick was hesitant as they entered what was once a grand stone-tiled hallway, but the tiles were worn, cracked and chipped. The hallway was devoid of any decor or mess other than wear and tear, but as soon as they stepped inside the first front room, the scene was quite different. Old furniture completely dominated the room, but was barely visible beneath files, papers and magazines. They stepped through a pathway of uncovered carpet to get a better look.

"It's more like a room where someone was sorting through stuff. I doubt he used it for relaxation," said Edna.

"It had been rented out before Jonny moved in. Maybe he took this stuff out of storage and was going through it before selling up."

Horace's eyes were sympathetic. "Why don't you check upstairs, Fred? We'll look around and see if we can make any sense of what's in here. I already checked the back room, and it's a dining room. The other front room's got a settee and two chairs, and is probably where he spent his evenings."

Sweat covered Frederick's forehead. He wiped it with another handkerchief. "I'm not sure we should be here at all."

"Your friend wanted you to be here. So now we are, let's have a look around for clues," Horace replied.

"I don't know. What if someone comes in?"

"Even if his family travel up from Cornwall today, it will take time for them to get ready. Driving that distance in July is not a quick journey," said Horace. "If there's any reason Jonny died except a natural one, we owe it to him and his family to find out what it was. That other rower mentioned his cousin, Michael."

"I agree with Horace," said Marjorie. "It's too much of a coincidence for Michael and Jonny to drown in the same spot."

"Not necessarily," said Edna. "If he felt guilty about this Michael's death, he might have wanted to go in the same way."

Marjorie glanced at Frederick before answering. "Edna makes a reasonable argument, but it could also turn out to be a killer's modus operandi."

"You read too many crime novels," said Edna.

Frederick's eyes were dull as he turned and reluctantly started up the stairs. "I'm not staying long."

"I'll help Frederick," Marjorie said.

"Good idea. Edna and I will go through some of this."

Once Frederick and Marjorie arrived on the dark landing, they tried a few of the bedroom doors. Curtains were pulled closed in all of them, but it was obvious which was the master bedroom because it was in the same state as the front room. Jonny had been trawling through old documents, either to get rid of them, or to search for something.

"Shall we start with the piles on the bed?" said Marjorie.

Frederick switched on the light, his eyes brightening as he looked around. "It's pretty obvious Jonny hadn't finished whatever his mission was, which discounts the suicide theory. It could still have been an accident I suppose."

"We'll keep an open mind for now. Was your friend always untidy?"

"Not when he lived in Bristol. Flora and I had dinner at his house a few times and I didn't notice anything out of the ordinary, but we're going back decades. He seemed depressed when we met up yesterday afternoon. I noticed his hair wasn't as neat as it used to be, but his clothes were."

Perhaps someone did his laundry. "Let's go with the idea that he was clearing and sorting through documents for now. I remember having to clear my parents' belongings after my father died. It was a daunting task." *Nothing like this*, Marjorie had to admit in her head, but if Jonny had only recently moved back to Henley and taken things from storage or out of a loft, it might explain it.

"Where did he sleep?" Frederick exclaimed. "The bed's swamped."

Marjorie pointed to a reclining chair with an empty glass and a half-full bottle of brandy on the nearby table. "It looks as if he was crashing there."

"Poor fellow. I should have visited after Judith died."

"You can't blame yourself," said Marjorie, trying to make sense of the piles of papers stacked on the bed. "Your friend Jonny seems to have sorted these piles in order. At least that's something. Most of them are bills going back years, that he was most likely going to shred. Were his parents hoarders?"

"I wouldn't know. He didn't talk much about his background when I knew him, other than how he came by the name Jonny. I can't even remember him mentioning he came from Henley; I always thought it was Oxford."

Frederick was becoming morose, staring at the reclining chair and not helping at all. Marjorie was pleased when Horace called upstairs.

"I think we've found something."

When they got downstairs, Edna was holding a small pile of newspapers in her hand and had a wide grin on her face. "That guy was right. Fred's friend was looking into the death of a chap called Michael Sebastian. These confirm he was found drowned in the River Thames, near to Henley Bridge."

Marjorie took a newspaper from Edna and read the headline out loud:

Local Rower Drowns!

Michael Sebastian, owner of Medionix Innovations in Henley, was fished from the River Thames this morning. First impressions are that he drowned after consuming a large quantity of alcohol...

"Sorry, Fred," said Edna. "It seems there's a pattern of behaviour developing here."

"There are a few more speculative articles in the local press suggesting he had a falling out with his rowing buddies the night before, after turning up to a training session drunk," said Horace. "Jonny's highlighted a couple of names."

Marjorie took another paper from Horace. "It says here that a Reginald Blackwood had refused to let him train with them on account of his drinking and that was the last he saw of him. There are also rumours Michael had a girlfriend, but his wife said it was nonsense and wouldn't speak to the reporter. She asked to be left alone. That's about the sum of it. Did Jonny mention any of this in his letters?" Marjorie asked Frederick.

Frederick shook his head. "Not a thing. I'm beginning to think I didn't know him at all and this might be a complete waste of his time, and now ours."

Marjorie was inclined to agree. Perhaps Frederick's friend had been unable to get over the death of his wife and had sought solace in alcohol – he wouldn't be the first – and under the influence created or imagined a conspiracy theory surrounding his cousin's death. *Except, he has now died in similar circumstances.*

"Is there a suicide note?" she asked Horace.

"No. I think we can assume his death wasn't suicide, but it doesn't rule out an accident. For all we know he could have been drinking all night. Sorry, Fred, Edna might be right about the pattern. He might have been drunk when he texted you and still drunk when he went to meet you."

"There's a half-empty bottle of brandy upstairs and the room reeks of the stuff," Frederick admitted.

"The kitchen's the same. Loads of empty spirit bottles in the bin and no signs of a person who looked after himself," said Horace.

Marjorie thought back to the brief encounter when Frederick had introduced them. Jonny had been smartly dressed and his beard and moustache neatly trimmed. He could clearly manage his outward appearance, apart from Frederick's mention of his unruly hair.

"It could have been an accident, but we all got the feeling Reginald wasn't being honest, and the man not only argued with Jonny the night before he drowned, he also did exactly the same with Michael. That's another pattern we should consider. We must speak to him again and, while we're at it, find out if Michael was having an affair and who with."

"Okay," said Frederick. "Now can we get out of here? It doesn't feel right being in a dead man's home."

"Look, Fred. Your mate wanted you to look around, which, like you said earlier, suggests he had an idea someone might do him in. So, before you go on a guilt trip, think on that."

"Edna's got a point," said Horace. "The least we can do is poke around and see what comes up. Do you think Jonny's volunteering at the regatta had more to do with the death of his cousin than his love of rowing?"

Frederick rubbed his forehead, eyes scrunched. "Possibly. He was much more into swimming than rowing when I knew him, and that Oswald chap said as much. Plus, he never mentioned rowing or the regatta in any of his letters. I also wonder why he was going to race today."

Marjorie was finding the house and all its papers and files overwhelming and didn't want Frederick to feel any more uncomfortable than he already did. "It appears the answer lies in his cousin's rowing history and with some of the people at the regatta. I suggest we go back there. Since you know Sir Andrew Eccles, Horace, perhaps you could speak to him and find out why he was so annoyed about Jonny being there. We can always come back here if we need to."

"Okay, I'll put the key back under the boulder and we can leave via the front door. Has anyone seen a front door key which we could leave under one of the stone statues?" said Horace.

"There's a key here," said Marjorie, lifting it from the hall table. She opened the front door and tried it. "Yes, it fits."

"Great," said Horace.

"Why not keep looking now?" Edna asked.

Horace glanced at Frederick. "Because it's a little too much at the moment, Edna."

Edna couldn't hide an exasperated sigh, but conceded. "Fine."

Marjorie assumed if they needed to come back, it would be without Frederick, whose heart wasn't in it. He had been happy to run into an old friend who, in the space of twenty-four hours, had turned out to have a drink problem and was now dead.

Horace chivvied them out of the house and it appeared he was just in time. After they had walked a short distance along the road, a police car passed them and turned into the driveway they had exited.

Horace blew out a breath. "That was close."

"Perhaps the pathologist has found something that warrants investigation." Marjorie had a growing feeling that Frederick's friend, for all his weaknesses, had died under suspicious circumstances.

"Are we calling a taxi or what?" Edna asked, panting after walking two hundred yards.

"Already done," said Horace. "It's picking us up at the lay-by just up the road."

NINE

As soon as they climbed into the taxi, Horace's phone pinged. He checked the message and sent a quick reply. "Looks like we'll have to skip the rest of the regatta today. Driver, please take us to Dinah's Hotel."

"Sure."

"What's going on?" Edna asked.

Horace passed his phone into the backseat. There was a message from Dinah.

> Two police officers are here wanting to speak to Frederick. Will you be back soon?

Horace's reply informed Dinah they were now on their way back to the hotel.

The two officers were waiting in the makeshift foyer. Marjorie recognised one of them from early that morning: the one whom she and Frederick had spoken to. She was with another officer wearing plain clothes.

"Hello again," the familiar officer smiled warmly, "I'm PC Trish Fry and this is Detective Constable Mark Briar. Mrs

Reynolds has kindly given us the use of her sitting room. Might we have a word with you, Mr Mackworth?"

"My friends are coming too," said Frederick, folding his arms.

PC Fry exchanged a look with the DC, who nodded.

When they entered the sitting room, they found Dinah had already laid out a tray with two pots of tea, a pot of coffee and a plateful of biscuits. The room was snug and welcoming like the rest of the hotel.

Edna helped herself to a chocolate biscuit. "I'll say something for your granddaughter, Horace. She knows what a woman needs after a long day."

It was mid-afternoon and Marjorie found the tea a welcome refreshment, and it gave them all something to occupy themselves with during the round of introductions. On closer inspection, PC Trish Fry appeared to be in her late twenties with keen blue eyes and blonde curls. The DC wasn't much older, a black man wearing a light grey suit with a starched white shirt and grey and black striped tie. A stubbly black moustache gave him the appearance of someone who wanted to look older than he was.

DC Briar cleared his throat before addressing Frederick. "You may have guessed, we are here about the death of your friend Mr Jonathan Sebastian."

"What have you found out?" Frederick asked.

"We are in the early stages of our enquiries. The pathologist will perform a post-mortem tomorrow morning. At the moment we're trying to establish his last movements and it appears you may have been the last person to see him alive."

Frederick gasped. "I hope you're not suggesting I had anything to do with his death?" Marjorie wished Frederick was better equipped to deal with stress. As it was, his face had turned bright red and his hands trembled.

"We're not suggesting anything yet, sir. Perhaps you could

tell us why you were so convinced this morning that the police should investigate Mr Sebastian's death as suspicious. Trish, erm... PC Fry said you were quite insistent."

Frederick's eyes pleaded with Marjorie's, but she didn't feel intervening on his behalf would do him any favours at present, so she just gave him a few words of encouragement.

"Tell them about the text."

"Right. When I woke this morning, I found a text from Jonny asking me to meet him before he started work. The text was sent in the middle of the night, last night."

"May we see it?" Briar asked.

Frederick unlocked his phone and showed them the message.

"Why do you think he wanted to meet you so urgently?"

"We'd met up by chance yesterday after not seeing each other for over twenty years, and we agreed to get together later for a beer. We went to university together and both had pharmacies in Bristol before Jonny moved to Cornwall."

Trish Fry arched an eyebrow as the two police officers shared a glance.

Briar spoke again. "So, you were a pharmacist?"

"We both were."

"I see. You were saying you met for drinks."

"Yes." Frederick was sweating. If the police suspected him of anything, he wasn't doing a lot to dissuade them. "We met for a pint and Jonny seemed out of sorts."

"In what way?" Trish Fry asked.

"He was drinking a lot and seemed moody. He could be moody at times."

"How do you know when you hadn't seen each other for" – Briar checked his notes – "over twenty years?"

Frederick wiped his brow. "He could get like that when I knew him, and his wife died a couple of years back. That in itself can make a man moody."

"You're a widower yourself, I understand," said Briar.

"What's that got to do with anything?" Frederick loosened his tie.

"I was merely inferring you might understand, empathise perhaps with his state of mind."

"Oh, I see. He told me he missed Judith and when I asked him what else was troubling him, all he would say was that he was in Henley on a mission."

Briar raised an eyebrow. "A mission?"

Marjorie didn't like the cynical tone she was hearing. If the police were here to tick a box, she had better enlighten them.

"We believe his purpose had something to do with the death of his cousin, Michael Sebastian. Michael himself drowned in similar circumstances some twenty years ago."

Trish wrote in her notepad. "Did he tell you this, Mr Mackworth?"

"No. I told you he wouldn't say. But—"

Marjorie jumped in again, afraid Frederick would tell the police they had been to Jonny's house. "We asked around this morning and one of the rowers mentioned it. Michael Sebastian was a keen rower who drowned in the very same spot where Frederick's friend Jonny was found this morning."

The two officers exchanged another glance before Trish asked, "You say you hadn't seen your friend for a long time, Mr Mackworth, and yet you imply his death is suspicious. Why?"

"Because he sent me a text in the middle of the night asking me to meet him early this morning. I believe he was going to tell me what he was doing in Henley."

"From our enquiries, we understand he was here to sell the family home."

"He mentioned that too, but he also said he was here to do something he should have done years ago."

"Like look into his cousin's death," said Edna. "Maybe you should be doing the same."

"If that was the case, why would he wait twenty years?" Briar asked.

"As I've already mentioned, Jonny's wife died a few years ago. It affected him badly. Losing a spouse makes you think about what's important."

Marjorie noted a watery eye as Frederick swiped at it. The four friends had all lost spouses and each one of them could relate to what Frederick was saying.

"Did he strike you as someone who might have become tired of life?" Trish asked.

"If you're asking whether my friend committed suicide, it crossed my mind, but it doesn't fit with his determination to look into his cousin's death or with his text to me."

"Could you give us the name of the person who suggested that's what he was doing in Henley?"

"I'm sorry, he didn't give us his name. He was one of the rowing team that won the over-fifties race. You could ask Reginald Blackwood or Oswald Greene about him. They were in the same team."

"Thank you. Could you tell us your whereabouts between midnight and six o'clock this morning?"

Frederick's eyes widened. He really would make a terrible criminal.

"I was here."

"Can anyone vouch for you?"

"We came back to the hotel together," said Horace. "And Frederick went to bed at the same time as the rest of us, around twelve-thirty."

"And I saw him leaving the hotel this morning shortly after six to meet his friend. That's when I joined him," said Marjorie.

Briar stood up. "Well, thank you for the information. We'll be in touch if we need anything else."

After the police left, the four helped themselves to a second round of hot drinks.

"They think I killed Jonny," said Frederick.

"Don't be stupid," said Edna. "If they thought that, they would have interviewed us separately, although you don't help yourself any. You looked guilty as hell even though we know you were telling the truth."

Marjorie sipped her tea before leaning back in the armchair. "Their working hypothesis is accident or suicide. Let's hope we've given them something else to think about."

"I got the impression they were just going through the motions," said Horace. "But as Marjorie says, if they're anywhere half decent at what they do, we've given them more to consider. They'll put what we've said together with what they find at Jonny's house and hopefully dig a little deeper."

"Let's hope the pathologist is thorough because I'm sure there will be evidence of foul play," added Marjorie.

"What do we do now?" Edna asked. "I don't feel like going back to the regatta today."

"I'd like to visit St Mary's Church," said Frederick.

"I meant about the investigation, but I suppose we could do with a bit of time off. If you lot are going to the church, I might go for a walk by the river."

"I'll keep you company," said Marjorie.

"In that case I'll go with Fred," said Horace. "Shall we meet back here for dinner?"

"Yes. And then I'd like an early night," said Marjorie.

"Fine. I'll let Dinah know."

TEN

Frederick would rather be on his own, but it would have been unkind to refuse Horace's company. As it turned out, he was finding Horace's easy-going way comforting and familiar.

St Mary's Church with its distinctive tower was at least easy to find. Horace had told Frederick on the way that the church had for a long time been central to the town's history and charm. They walked up the path and found it nestled beside the River Thames.

They walked around the churchyard for a while, studying the weather-worn gravestones that went back centuries. Ancient yews had become twisted and gnarled with age.

Frederick was studying one gravestone in particular, one with an interesting marking, when the doors of the church opened and people exited. A man approached them.

"That belongs to a seventeenth-century priest. Rumour has it the marking is that of a serpent wrapped around a cross."

Frederick couldn't quite see the resemblance, but he wasn't arty.

"I can see why," said Horace.

"I believe it's linked to a cult that once operated in Henley. Most people say that's mumbo-jumbo, but I find it interesting to postulate."

"Is the church open to visitors?" Frederick asked, feeling a shiver run down his spine.

"I don't see why not. We've just finished a Bible study. You'll find Sylvia inside, she's a local and has studied the history of the church." The man touched his nose, leaning in. "She loves showing off her knowledge but don't believe everything she tells you. Like me, she likes to fill in the gaps with her own theories. Tell her you've spoken to Harold."

"Thanks," said Horace. "We will."

Frederick took another cautious glance around the graveyard. He didn't know what had drawn him to look at the headstones in the first place, but now they, and the yews, were giving him the creeps. He'd had enough of death for one day.

"Maybe we should go back to the hotel."

"Come on, Fred, it will take your mind off things." Horace was already heading towards the open door.

"As long as she doesn't mention spooks and stuff." Frederick normally liked folklore but today wasn't the day.

"I'll move her off the topic, should it come up."

They stepped inside through the open door. The cooler air was refreshing after the heat from outside. Henley's heatwave was burning Frederick's cheeks whereas Horace was sporting a healthy tan, but he was used to foreign holidays and had a Romanian mother whose genes may have been protecting him from the fierce rays. Frederick made a mental note to pick up some sunscreen on the way back to the hotel.

There was a faint whiff of incense in the air, but the smell was mostly of stone and the church's history. Did history have a smell? It seemed that way sometimes.

Frederick's eyes were drawn upwards where high vaulted

ceilings with wooden beams seemed to add warmth to the otherwise cold stone interior. Sunlight was filtering inside from tall arched stained-glass windows. It cast vibrant patches of colour across the flagstone floor. It even added reds, blues, and greens to some of the pews.

Horace was meandering around. "I've been to Henley many times but can't say I've ever been inside this place."

They heard a sound of quiet sobbing coming from a pew in front of the nave. A woman was sitting with her head bowed, crying into a handkerchief.

"We should go," said Frederick.

Horace ignored him and continued on his way, making sure he made a noise to warn the woman she wasn't alone. Her head swung around.

"I thought everyone had gone," she said, swiping at the tears before standing up.

"Sorry to bother you. We met a chap outside called Harold and told him we were interested in the church's history. He suggested we look for a lady called Sylvia."

"You've found her. I'm Sylvia Swann."

"Look, if it's not a good time, we can leave," said Frederick.

Sylvia Swann steadied herself and straightened up. She was around sixty, tall and skinny with spiky grey hair. Her clothes were designer and when she picked up her clipboard, Frederick realised he'd seen her before. This was the woman who had warned Jonny to go easy on the drink the evening before.

"There's no need," she said. "I love this place and can talk about it all day."

"I'm Horace and this is Fred. I understand the church is fifteenth century," said Horace.

"It actually dates back to the thirteenth century according to records, but most of what you see today was rebuilt in the fifteenth century. That's when the tower was added."

Horace blew out a whistle. "I bet it has seen some things in its lifetime."

"Quite so. The tower is a landmark that can be seen from miles around. We have a great set of bells that calls people to church and has done for centuries. The story is that they were rehung following the English Civil War in the seventeenth century. There are folklore rumours that, after 1752, when they buried the infamous 'poisoner of Henley', Mary Blandy, following her execution, in the churchyard, people heard strange reverberations at odd hours. They reckoned the bells were rung by spirits of the dead complaining about having a murderer in their midst."

Frederick swallowed hard, looking upwards. "The bells don't do that anymore, do they?"

Sylvia grinned. "No. And I don't believe they did it back then either, but some of our more superstitious residents continue to tell ghost stories. They also say Mary Blandy walks around parts of Henley."

"Is that archway gothic?"

Frederick was grateful for Horace keeping his promise. He was pointing to the archway framing the chancel.

"Yes, it is."

"I love the stained glass," said Frederick. There was a window over the communion table depicting Jesus Christ and others, most likely saints.

"We think it's Victorian in design. The church was remodelled in the fifteenth and nineteenth centuries. St Leonard's Chapel is the oldest part."

"I guess a place like this has seen a lot of history. It's a shame we can't ask the building itself," said Horace.

"Wouldn't that be good. I could write a book on the rumours that flow through Henley about this building. But for me, it's a place of worship and solace."

"As it should be," said Horace.

"The most famous memorial outside – and the most visited – belongs to Dusty Springfield. Some of her ashes were buried in the churchyard. I'm sure you remember her?"

"Yes. I still have the single record of *I Only Want To Be With You*," said Horace.

"Anyway, I'd give you a tour of the church but I need to lock up before meeting some friends at the regatta."

"Oh. We're staying in Henley for the regatta ourselves," said Horace. "I used to come for business but this trip is for pleasure."

"I think I recognise you," said Frederick. "You were talking to Jonny Sebastian yesterday afternoon."

The tension in Sylvia's jaw was immediate and she clicked her pen repeatedly, the sound echoing through the church. "I spoke to a lot of people yesterday. In fact, I used to be a pundit for the races so I know almost everybody. Sorry, I don't recognise you." She was looking at Horace.

"We couldn't help noticing you were upset about something when we came in," said Frederick. "I take it you heard Jonny drowned?"

Tears threatened to flow once more but Sylvia blinked them away. The pen was clicking faster than a speedboat.

"It brought back memories, that's all."

"Of Michael," said Frederick.

Sylvia paused the pen-clicking for a moment before setting it off again and hugging the clipboard to her chest. "I really must ask you to leave. As I said, I'm late."

"But—"

Frederick felt Horace tug at his arm. "Come along, Fred. Sylvia has given us enough of her time. Thank you," he said to Sylvia, who turned away to face the altar.

Once outside, Frederick turned on Horace. "Why did you do that? She knows something."

"She knew Michael. That much was obvious. Perhaps she

was the lover mentioned in the paper, but I'm not in the habit of harassing upset ladies, especially not in the house of God. Think how upset you were this morning."

"You're right. I bet she's the one mentioned in the papers."

The streets of Henley were much busier as they made their way back to the hotel, Frederick with a lot on his mind.

ELEVEN

"Thank you for meeting me, Andrew," said Horace.

"It's been a long time, but now I remember who you are. You're looking good, Horace." Sir Andrew Eccles pulled out a chair at the Fawley Bar & Awning, and waved a bartender over. "Drink?"

"Just a soda water for me, thanks," said Horace.

It was the third day of the regatta and Horace was keeping his promise to talk to Sir Andrew. The bartender had a brief conversation with the man, who ordered a glass of Pimm's and a soda water, then went to the bar, returning moments later with their drinks. There was a general hubbub of conversation going on all around them and a lot of laughter.

Andrew looked up from his Pimm's. "It's good to catch up and all that, but you said on the phone you wanted to talk to me about something specific. How can I help?"

Straight to the point and probably not pleased to catch up at all, Horace concluded. He had been remembering their previous meetings since Frederick did his Wiki search. Andrew had, in the past, bought components from Tyler Avionics to adapt for some of his boat engines. His had been small business compared to the usual contracts Horace's company engaged in, but his links to the regatta had made it convenient for Horace to deal with him.

Now that Horace was sitting opposite the man, he hesitated to bring up the subject. "It's been quite a while since I've visited the regatta. I'm retired, apart from remaining on the board. My sons enjoy the sailing and they bring overseas guests here from time to time."

"I've been here every year for as far back as I can remember. It's never been about business to me." Andrew would not be a person Horace could call a friend, hence him not immediately recalling his name. But whenever they had met in the past for business or in passing, he had been relatively easy to get along with, albeit always a bit on the curt side. The same couldn't be said now. There was an impatient edge to Andrew's voice that wouldn't have been there before. But then, that was business.

Horace finished his glass of soda and wiped his mouth, before inhaling through his nose. "I'm only here this year because of friends. One of them is an ex-pharmacist named Frederick Mackworth. The day before yesterday, he was reunited with an old pal from university. They'd kept in touch over the years but hadn't seen each other in some time."

Andrew sat back while the waiter brought him another Pimm's before saying anything. "That's all very interesting, but what is it you want to talk to me about?"

"The man Frederick was reunited with died yesterday morning."

A flicker of recognition crossed Andrew's brow and the slight neck flush was a giveaway. "Jonathan Sebastian?"

"That's the man. One of my company, Lady Marjorie Snellthorpe, thought she saw you glowering at Mr Sebastian on the day we arrived, and she and Frederick observed you when his body was pulled from the river."

"There was a group of gawkers there, I cleared them off. So, yes, I was there when he was pulled out. A young rowing team found the body. Kids from a local college. I was taking a walk when I heard the commotion. The police were there by then. But as for any glowering, your friend is mistaken. I hardly knew Jonathan Sebastian."

"Are you sure about that? Lady Marjorie has a keen eye for detail and, in my experience, is rarely mistaken."

"That might be the case, Horace, but I assure you that on this occasion, she is. When was this supposed glowering anyway?"

"Not long after we arrived at the regatta, on the first day as a matter of fact. We were having drinks in the Coffee and Ices Garden."

"I was there early on, checking some things, but I didn't notice you. I'd have said hello if I had."

I doubt that. "Lady Marjorie thought you were distracted by Jonny Sebastian's presence."

"Look, Horace, I don't know what you or your friend are implying, but she's made a mistake. I met the chap years ago when he rowed, but he was nothing to me."

"You could be right. We're none of us getting any younger. Did you know his cousin, Michael?"

Andrew had relaxed, but at the mention of Michael, his jaw tensed and his lips tightened. "Where's all this coming from?"

"Jonny mentioned the death of his cousin to my friend Frederick, when they met for a drink towards the end of the first day. Jonny believed Michael's death was suspicious and was determined to find out what happened." A little white lie couldn't do any harm, and judging by Andrew's reaction, it was paying dividends.

Redness climbed Andrew's neck like a rash. He swallowed hard before answering. "I met Michael Sebastian and knew him by reputation. I didn't like him if I'm honest. He knew Elsa and

Sylvia back in the day. A flagrant flirt and a ladies' man, but I don't like to speak ill of the dead."

Horace and Frederick's suspicions that Sylvia might be Michael's former lover could be right. "Can you give me more details? It might be important."

"The word on the street was to keep your wives locked up when Michael Sebastian was around. He was married but that didn't stop him philandering."

"I take it his wife died?"

"Not as far as I know. She remarried and moved abroad. You might be better off speaking to Elsa. She knew both Sebastians and the rest of the family."

"Who is this Elsa?" Horace asked.

"Dr Elsa Christie. She was the regatta doctor back in Michael's day and a local GP. She's retired now, but still keeps her hand in. If you ask around, you'll find her; she attends the regatta every day. You might be best looking in or around the first aid tent."

"What about the other woman you mentioned, Sylvia?" Horace wanted to do a little bit of fishing.

"She was a racing pundit. I think she and Michael might have had a fling but I can't be sure. You'll find her around as well. Tall woman with spiky hair."

"Thanks, Andrew. There is just one more thing. Do you remember anything about Michael Sebastian's death?"

The redness reappeared as he finished up his drink and smacked the plastic glass down on the table before getting up. "How could I forget? It was me who found the body. Sorry, Horace, you're going to have to excuse me. I've got things to do."

After dropping his bombshell, Andrew left Horace rubbing his head as well as footing the bill. Andrew had never been one to pay his way, despite his wealth.

"You look as though you heard something interesting," said

Marjorie, who appeared with Fred moments after Andrew left. They both took seats at the table.

"Where did you two come from?"

"We were hovering over there, watching on," said Fred, gesturing with his hand. "It seemed pally enough until you got to the point."

"You're on the right track, Fred. It's the past we need to delve into. Whatever hornet's nest Jonny stirred up, I think it was about Michael Sebastian."

At that moment they heard shouting and screaming coming from the far end of the enclosure. Edna's voice was unmistakable. Horace was up first, hurrying through the crowds towards the noise.

"Get them away from me!"

"Calm down, madam. You're making it worse." A portly man had covered Edna with a large blazer while another man dressed in a white beekeeper's outfit shook his head, muttering to himself.

"Get them away from me! Do you hear me?"

"They're gone," the man spoke calmly. "If you would just stay still."

"What happened?" Horace asked.

"Do you know this lady?"

"Yes." Horace saw a few red blotches on the man's face and hands.

"In that case, I'll leave her in your capable hands." The portly man removed his blazer from Edna's shoulders and shook it out before returning to a group of people having a picnic by the river.

"I take it you encountered a few bees?" Marjorie said, her bright blue eyes twinkling in the sunlight.

"A few! I tell you, Marge, there were thousands. I'm lucky to be alive."

The man who had suffered the bee stings was gesturing

towards Edna, telling the story to his friends who were laughing. Horace took her arm.

"Let's get you away from here. Perhaps a glass of champagne will help your recovery."

"Did you get stung?" Marjorie asked, examining Edna.

"No. When they came at me, I ducked behind that bloke back there who covered me with his blazer. Good job he's so big or it wouldn't have protected me. See, there are advantages to being overweight."

"I doubt he'd see being stung by bees as an advantage," murmured Fred.

"The noise must have attracted the beekeeper who came along and sorted them out."

Horace snorted a laugh.

"What's so funny, Horace Tyler?"

"You're the only person I know, Edna Parkinton, who can disturb a beehive and escape unscathed."

"Unscathed? I'm scarred for life. You have no idea the trauma I suffered while you were swanning off for drinks with your old mate, Sir Andrew Fuddy-Duddy."

"What about that poor man's trauma?" said Marjorie, pointing back towards Edna's rescuer. "It's a good thing he isn't allergic to bee stings."

"He'll be all right. He told me a crocodile had once bitten him."

Marjorie chuckled. "Which you believed, I suppose."

"Now you mention it, he might have been trying to shut me up. I tend to yell when I get attacked, especially by a swarm of bees."

Ten at most, thought Horace, remembering the beekeeper who'd had around four on his suit.

"You should be more careful, Edna," said Fred. "We need our bees and every one that stung that man will have died."

Horace grabbed Edna's arm and steered her towards the

Fawley Bar, ordering a glass of champagne before she took a bite out of Fred.

"Some people don't seem to care that I almost died out there," Edna snapped, glaring at Fred.

"Perhaps when you've calmed down, you could tell us what you were doing over there in the first place," said Marjorie. "I believe that area has a sign saying it's closed to the public."

"If you must know, I was following that Reggie fella. He was behaving suspiciously."

"Stealing honey, I suppose," muttered Fred.

Horace grinned and Marjorie laughed, but thankfully Edna hadn't heard, focussing her full attention on the bubbly contents of her glass.

"I suggest we go somewhere quieter to share our findings," Horace said.

"Any suggestions?" Marjorie asked, gazing at the crowds teeming all around them.

"It would probably be quiet near the hives if Edna could show us where she was," said Fred.

"Are you bonkers? I wouldn't go back there if my life depended on it."

Horace took her hand. "He's teasing, Edna. We could go back to Dinah's or we could get a table outside in the Little Lion Meadow. It's quieter at this time of day."

"Or we could stay here," suggested Fred, folding his arms triumphantly.

Horace watched people leaving the tent in droves, before hearing an announcement that a big race featuring Olympic rowers was about to start. People were flocking out of all the hospitality tents and gardens to the grandstand or the river.

"Oh, how exciting. I'd much rather watch the race," said Marjorie.

Edna huffed so loud her face went purple as she pointed at

Fred. "Then *he* shouldn't drag us into murder investigations, should he?"

"I'm sure we can do both. Where are the multitasking abilities you're always telling us about?" said Marjorie. "Watching Olympians row in the flesh is a once in a lifetime opportunity. Murder can wait."

Horace grinned. "I've just seen Prince Michael of Kent take a seat in the stands."

Edna's interest was aroused. "Where?"

Horace pointed to an entourage in the front seats of the main grandstand. "If you look closely, you'll see a few celebrities up there as well."

"Hand me your binoculars, Fred," Edna commanded.

Fred did as he was asked. "The race is that way," he muttered, pointing in the opposite direction to where Edna trained the lenses.

"Let's hurry or we'll miss it." Marjorie nudged Edna, who reluctantly handed Fred's binoculars back to him.

They turned to follow the crowds heading towards the riverbank as the atmosphere became more charged. It was electric and Horace found himself enjoying the regatta this year far more than he had ever done when it was all about business.

Edna lagged behind. "Come on, old girl," he said. "We can talk murder later, let's have a bit of fun."

"Only if you get me another one of these," Edna retorted, holding up her empty glass.

"I promise I'll get you another over lunch, after the race."

They followed Marjorie and Fred to their reserved deckchairs, while the Olympic rowers came their way, urged on by the cheerful shouts of those watching from both sides of the river and the grandstands.

TWELVE

Marjorie had enjoyed the race and the dedication and speed of the rowers so much that she'd almost forgotten about Jonny Sebastian's demise. With multitudes of people enjoying a rare British heatwave at the Henley Royal Regatta, it was hard to imagine that a man had lost his life in the same river the boats sped along. All too aware of Frederick fidgeting in the deckchair to her right, she turned to Horace in the one to her left.

"As much as I'd love to stay and watch some more, we ought to find somewhere to chat."

"Righto. It's lunchtime anyway." Horace gently nudged Edna who was on his left, dozing but thankfully not snoring. "Time to go, Edna."

"Already? I've just got comfortable." She rubbed sleep from her eyes.

"Where to?" asked Frederick.

"The Luncheon Tent."

"Come on, Edna. Let me help you." Horace offered her a hand, which she took.

Once settled in the tent, they were soon enjoying starters. People were filling the tables, ready for the delicious lunches they were being served each day. Marjorie checked around to make sure no-one was listening to them, then turned to Edna before she started munching on pâté and toast.

"I don't want to reignite your bee trauma, but you mentioned following Reginald because he was acting suspiciously. What did you mean?" Marjorie placed a napkin on her knee and began eating her prawn cocktail.

"It was the way he skulked away from the main enclosure. You're right about the 'not open to the public' notice. But he was looking shifty before he headed that way, so I followed. I scuffed the heel of my shoe, which means I'll need a new pair. I wonder if I can get the regatta people to buy me a pair, seeing as a swarm of their bees chased me."

Frederick rolled his eyes while taking a mouthful of soup.

"As you were in a place you shouldn't have been in, I doubt it," said Marjorie. "Now could we get back to the topic in hand?"

Edna huffed, glancing down at the scuffed heel before saying anything else. "It's not fair. I bought these specially for the occasion."

"Don't worry, Edna. I'm sure we can get them repaired. If not, I'll buy you a new pair," said Horace.

Edna beamed. "I saw a shoe shop on the main street."

Frederick sighed, but Marjorie shot him a warning look before turning to Edna again.

"That's wonderful. Now back to Reginald Blackwood."

"Oh yeah." Edna could resist her pâté no longer and took a large bite of toast before continuing. "Well, he met with that coach bloke, Ossie, and a prim woman wearing a pink skirt suit."

Marjorie's interest was piqued. "That sounds like the woman Sir Andrew complained to about Jonny on the day we arrived. Did you hear what they were saying?"

"No. They disappeared along a hedge-lined path, and when

I tried to follow, I tripped. I think that's when I scuffed my shoe, then I bumped into something." Edna shuddered.

Horace patted her on the arm. "The edge of a beehive, I take it."

"You know the rest. The bees attacked me and I was traumatised."

Frederick poured himself a glass of water, saying, "You were lucky you didn't fall into it or—"

"Quite." Marjorie noted the look of sheer terror on Edna's face. "I wonder what the three of them were meeting about." She took a sip of her own water.

"It might have been something to do with the racing, it sounds like they're all part of the in-crowd," said Frederick bitterly.

"I'm not sure my chat with Andrew was all that useful," said Horace, "but it definitely struck a chord when I mentioned Michael."

They were temporarily interrupted as their starter plates were cleared away and main courses arrived. The aroma from Horace's and Edna's steaks was tempting, but Marjorie had opted for a chicken salad while Frederick was trying a pasta dish.

"Did Sir Andrew say what he was doing in the vicinity when Jonny was found?" asked Frederick.

"I think he said he was taking an early morning walk. I got the impression he knows something, but he clammed up, even more so when I mentioned Michael, who was apparently a womaniser."

"I expect your Sir Andy Pandy was jealous of him," said Edna. "You men are all the same if you ask me."

"We're not," said Frederick, almost choking on his pasta. He swallowed it down. "And that remark is sexist. What would you say if I made a sweeping generalisation like that?"

"Everyone's entitled to their opinion. That's the trouble these days—"

"Opinions are one thing, Edna. Double standards are something else. Frederick is quite right, you would rip him to shreds if he said anything like you've just said."

"Have it your way, Marge." Edna cut a large chunk of steak and put the whole lot in her mouth.

Horace grinned before continuing. "Andrew came across as quite angry about Michael's habits. He said that men were warned to keep their wives out of sight around him. It made me wonder if Michael Sebastian was seeing Andrew's wife."

"I doubt it if she lived in Norfolk, but if he was, it would give Sir Andrew a motive for killing both men. One out of jealousy and the other to prevent word getting out. What did he say about Jonny?" Marjorie quizzed.

"He said their paths had crossed but denied knowing him well. He also insisted that you were wrong about his being angry that Jonny was at the regatta."

"Interesting," said Marjorie. "He could well be our chief suspect. Why deny it? We should speak to the woman in the pink suit Edna was following. She should be able to corroborate my story."

"Andrew also mentioned Michael knowing Sylvia – the lady Fred and I met in St Mary's yesterday – but he wasn't sure if they were having an affair. The other person he suggested speaking to is a retired doctor called Elsa Christie. Apparently, Michael was friendly with her as she was a local GP for many years."

"Good work, Horace," said Marjorie. "It seems to me your conversation was far more productive than you thought."

Horace beamed. "You're right, but the most interesting part is yet to come."

"Go on then. Don't keep us in suspense," said Edna in between mouthfuls.

"Sir Andrew Eccles found Michael Sebastian's body."

Frederick glowered. "That's too much of a coincidence. He's got to be the killer."

Marjorie steepled her hands under her chin. "It's certainly an interesting development, but far from conclusive."

"We know he didn't like Jonny," Horace said, "and his wife could have been seeing the cousin Michael."

"That's enough for me," said Edna.

"It's pretty damning," Frederick added.

"And yet," said Marjorie, "in my limited experience, a murderer isn't the one to find the body of the person they killed, and certainly not twice. He might have a spurious motive, but so far even that isn't proven."

"He didn't find Jonny's body," said Frederick, "rowers did."

"Nevertheless, he came forward rather than making himself scarce," Marjorie countered. "Although, now I think of it, his trousers were wet and his shoes muddy. The woman I spoke to said he hadn't been involved in bringing the body out, something Frederick and I witnessed ourselves."

"I didn't notice the trousers and shoes," said Frederick.

"Your attention was on your friend and the police," said Marjorie.

"Andrew appears arrogant enough to think he can do what he likes," said Horace. "I've just remembered another reason I didn't take to him. It was his sense of entitlement. He wasn't born a sir, but I bet he made the most of it once he was made one."

"My observations of the man make me inclined to agree with you, but we need more than intuition and dislike to prove he had anything to do with either death," said Marjorie.

"You've just said his trousers were wet," said Edna, putting her knife and fork together.

"True and we need to ask how that happened. But there's

also the secret meeting you observed, and Reginald Blackwood certainly isn't being honest."

"Private doesn't mean secret," said Frederick. "Although I agree Reginald is hiding something. Why didn't he mention Michael? Now I think about it, I bet it was his death he was telling Jonny to drop."

"Let's go over what we've discovered so far," said Marjorie.

"A load of conjecture if you ask me," said Edna. "Apart from Sir Andy Bloomin' Eccles. We still don't know whether either of the two deaths are murder. Some families are cursed, you know. It might have been fate caused them both to drown in the same river near the same bridge."

Frederick's brow furrowed. "This is not fate. Jonny wanted to tell me something and I'm going to find out what it was. With or without your help."

"Okay. No need to get in a sulk about it. I'm just saying if it isn't the obvious Sir Full-of-Himself, we've got no other proof."

"Which is why we're going to help Fred get it," said Horace. "You were going to summarise, Marjorie?"

"As I was saying, so far, we have two dead men, both seemingly the victims of accidental drowning, and – as Edna points out – they died in more or less the same place, but twenty years apart. The first, Michael Sebastian, was an amateur rower and a business owner, but we don't yet know whether his day job had anything to do with rowing. We know that Michael had been drinking heavily the night before his death—"

"Like Jonny," Edna interrupted.

"Indeed. Back to Michael. He was most likely having an affair with Sylvia Swann, who Frederick and Horace met yesterday and Sir Andrew mentioned. The other avenue to follow is that this is a rowing community and our suspects are involved in or linked to the regatta. Is there a connection here?"

"Corruption, you mean?" Horace asked. "I doubt it. The regatta's got a sterling reputation."

"We'll keep an open mind on that."

"If foul play is and was involved, the killer had to make sure there was no evidence for a pathologist to find," said Frederick.

"Suspect list?" asked Horace.

"Sir Andrew Eccles is at the top of mine."

"In which case, he's at the bottom of mine, 'cos you're rarely right, Fred," Edna countered.

"We've also got Reginald Blackwood who warned Jonny to back off and wanted him out of Henley," added Frederick, ignoring Edna's barb.

"Then there's the former coach Oswald Greene, and the woman in pink who we haven't spoken to yet. We need her to enlighten us on why Sir Andrew was annoyed by Jonny's presence."

"And there's the doctor Horace mentioned. Doctors would know how to make deaths look accidental, wouldn't they?" Edna said. "Plus, this Sylvia Swann woman who you both said was upset yesterday."

Horace poured them all second cups of tea. "I can't see it being her. And there's also Michael's widow. Maybe she wasn't happy with his philandering. Andrew said she remarried and moved abroad."

"You didn't mention her before," said Edna.

"I forgot."

"It's by the by," said Frederick. "Unless she's come back to Henley to drown Jonny – which I very much doubt – it's not her."

Marjorie agreed, but made a mental note to establish the whereabouts of the ex-Mrs Michael Sebastian. "I suggest Horace and I have another chat with Reginald and Oswald. Because Horace is a member of the same club, he will be given more respect—"

"And you're titled, Marge, so you'll fit in with the old boys' network," Edna added, not too bitterly for a change.

"I could have a chat with the doctor. My wife was a doctor," said Frederick. "I can say I heard she and Michael were friends and that Jonny mentioned something about him."

"That's the line I took with Andrew," said Horace.

"What am I going to do while you're all hobnobbing with the high and mighty?" Edna asked.

"See if you can have a word with the lady in pink and do a little flirting with Andrew. Michael wasn't the only one who liked a pretty face," Horace said.

"Do you really think I'm pretty?"

"Of course you are. Sir Andrew Eccles will be putty in your hands."

Marjorie scrutinised Edna. Although she carried too much weight, she dressed well and was always made up as if she was about to go on stage and belt out her favourite Shirley Bassey number. She looked younger than her eighty-odd years and the new wig bought especially for the regatta added to her attractive looks.

"How will I introduce myself?" Edna said, pouting.

"Spilling a drink is always a good ploy. Failing that you could give him a wink with those big brown eyes," Horace said, chuckling.

"Or stir up a hornet's nest," added Marjorie.

"Ha... bloomin'... ha, Marge. I'd like to see you deal with a swarm of bees."

Frederick opened his mouth, but snapped it shut again when Marjorie once more shook her head.

"You could just ask him for directions. I always find that works when I want to speak to someone I don't know," said Horace.

"It's a shame your Sir Andrew isn't gay, because you're the biggest flirt of them all if you ask me," said Edna, snorting.

"Along with the fact I've already spoken to him and we don't really like each other."

"And that," Edna agreed. "I've got another suggestion."

"I know what you're going to say, but say it anyway," said Marjorie.

"Why don't we... or Fred... tell the police what we've found out and add in our... his... suspicions?"

"She's got a point," said Frederick.

"It would be better if we had more to tell them, and I wouldn't know how to contact them again seeing as they didn't give us a card," said Marjorie.

"I don't know if you've noticed, Marge, but there are hundreds of cops walking around the regatta."

Marjorie had noticed some, but after the response of the two police officers to what they were told yesterday, she wasn't ready to do battle with them yet.

"They wouldn't listen yesterday," said Frederick, as if reading Marjorie's thoughts. "Perhaps we should do a little more work ourselves and then contact them."

Edna blew out her cheeks. "Fine. I'll take Sir Andrew Flippin' Narcissist first, then see if I can track down the woman in pink. We're going to miss the afternoon's racing if we don't hurry."

As Marjorie watched Edna go, she wondered if it might be better to flag down one of the officers in attendance and ask them to contact DC Briar or PC Fry. If she saw either of them, she would be happy to share what they had found out. Somehow, though, she felt convinced it would be better to gather more evidence first.

"Frederick, when you track down Dr Christie, why don't you ask her if she can have a word with the pathologist or coroner about Jonny?"

"I will. And if she won't, I'll speak to Jonny's daughter. I'm sure I've got her details somewhere. We could always go back to Jonny's and see if the family has arrived."

Marjorie nodded. "Good plan. First, though, Horace and I

will track down Reginald and/or Oswald, and try to confirm our suspicions that Sylvia Swann was Michael's rumoured girlfriend. It could be significant."

THIRTEEN

Horace strode confidently towards the boathouses and spoke to a couple of people who were moving boats around before returning to Marjorie. "Oswald's at the starting line, but they say Reginald should be back soon."

"I suggest we wait here for Reginald. Even if we took a water taxi to the starting line, Oswald could be gone by the time we got there."

Horace's eyes turned back towards the boathouses. "Good plan, let's wait here."

Marjorie and Horace stood at a discreet distance while ensuring they were able to watch people entering and exiting the boat storage area. Horace explained to Marjorie how clubs or the rowers themselves serviced and maintained the boats, depending on budgets and numbers.

"I assume most of the boats are moved once the racing's over?"

"Yes. If they're only here for one race, they will be transported back whence they came, be it a college or a boat club. Some of those rowed by professionals go back to where they practise or move on to the next competition."

How privileged they had already been to see so many races over the first few days, with many more to follow. Marjorie was smiling happily when a gruff voice jarred her from her musings.

"I hear you're looking for me."

Marjorie turned her head to see Reginald Blackwood marching towards them. His windswept hair and the sweat dripping from his sideburns suggested he had been working outdoors.

"We are," said Horace. "You look hot. Can we buy you a drink?"

Momentarily disarmed, Reginald lost his scowl. "Okay. But I don't have long." The man scrutinised his Rolex wristwatch. An odd thing to wear if he'd been exercising.

Once they were in the Beer Garden, Horace's easy-going manner worked its magic and, with a pint of draught ale in his left hand, Reginald soon relaxed. Marjorie enjoyed the taste of real lemonade rather than real ale. She wasn't a beer drinker and would look forward to a glass of wine with dinner.

Watching Reginald Blackwood gulp back his ale, Marjorie said, "Please accept our apologies if we caught you at a bad time yesterday. We should have allowed you to savour your well-deserved victory."

"What? Oh yes. Thanks." Reginald flashed a wide grin revealing overly white teeth. "It's been a while since I rowed competitively. I wasn't sure I'd get through the race, let alone be on the winning team, but we did it."

"From what I saw, you still have the knack," said Horace. "Cheers." He held up his glass.

"Cheers," said Reginald, slugging back another large mouthful. "And thanks. I guess rowing's like riding a bike. Once I got into the rhythm, it all came back to me."

Observing Reginald devouring his beer, Marjorie wondered if fast drinking was another one of the boating community's rituals. "We're enjoying watching the races. It must be wonderful living in a town where an annual world-renowned event takes place."

"It has its perks," said Reginald. "I always take the week off work to help out in any way I can."

"That's kind of you. We understand you work as an estate agent," Marjorie said.

"How would you know that?"

"Jonny Sebastian mentioned it to our friend Frederick."

"What else did Jonny mention?" The sour look returned.

"Just that you were an old family friend and that you knew his cousin Michael. We hear he drowned under similar circumstances to Jonny some twenty years ago." Marjorie eyed Reginald closely as he fiddled with his tie.

"I've been thinking about that since yesterday. It's weird, isn't it? Does your friend think Jonny took his own life? He wasn't the man I remember, but it's been a long time since he lived in Henley and the place has changed a lot. He used to visit once or twice a year when his parents were alive, but since being back... Well..." Reginald took another gulp of beer.

"Well, what?" Marjorie asked.

"He's been down. Moody and moping around. I didn't even realise he'd volunteered to row in a race, let alone help with the regatta until a few days ago."

Horace dropped his bombshell. "We believe he was looking into Michael's death, and that he didn't think it was an accident."

Reginald's face reddened. "Mere conspiracy theories and rumours. Henley is full of them, but you're right, Jonny was going around upsetting everyone Michael had known. Throwing wild accusations at people who don't deserve it. I bet he didn't tell your friend he had a drink problem?" Reginald spat the words out, slamming his glass down on the table with a thud. Marjorie was pleased it was plastic. A few people turned to look, but soon returned to their conversations.

Horace remained calming. "People rarely admit to such things, but Frederick noticed Jonny was drinking heavily. He was sober when we were introduced to him a couple of days ago, though."

"Was his drinking the reason you argued with him?" Marjorie pressed.

"Look, Lady Snellthorpe, ever since Jonny arrived back here, he's been like an irritating fly buzzing around the town. First, he upset Sylvia, then Elsa, and then most people started avoiding him. I'm certain he only joined the rowing club to spread rumours. I liked his cousin Michael, but his death was an accident and that's all there was to it.

"Like I said, people had had enough of Jonny. Sir Andrew Eccles was annoyed about Jonny volunteering to help out with the regatta. He's a generous benefactor of one of the local schools, and I thought it was time someone told Jonny to get out of Dodge. So, in answer to your question, I wasn't so much bothered about his drinking, more about his attitude to people who lived here."

"How did he take your suggestion to get out of Dodge, as you put it?" Horace quizzed.

"I didn't wait to find out. I left him to think it over."

"Someone suggested you wanted to add his parents' home to your sales list," said Marjorie.

"Is that what he told your friend? What kind of world do you live in? You think I threw him in the river to get a sale? I don't need the business, and even if I did, that's not the way I'd go about things. Jonny would need to be alive if I were to put that house on my list. There's no guarantee his family will want to sell the place, they might decide to keep it. Either way, it'll be months in probate. If you want to look into my company, feel free. I have nothing to hide. It's thriving, Lady Marjorie. I don't know what you've heard about estate agents, but we don't go around killing people to sell houses!" With that sentence finished, Reginald threw back more ale.

"I didn't imagine you did," Marjorie said, flashing what she hoped was a disarming smile. "But let me ask you this. Are you certain both men's deaths were accidental?"

Reginald took a quick look around before answering quietly. "I can't see how they could have been anything else."

"But you're not convinced," said Horace.

"Like I said before, it's been on my mind a lot since I heard Jonny had gone. It's a horrible coincidence, but stranger things happen."

"Frederick assures us Jonny was a strong swimmer who went wild water swimming," said Marjorie. "Oswald mentioned seeing him."

"He's right, Jonny was when sober. I also saw him in the Thames when I took my boat out."

"I thought you were out of practice?"

Reginald met her eye to eye for the first time since they had sat down, his eyebrows knitted together. "I said I hadn't raced for a long time. That's different. Lots of people who live along the riverbank own boats and I'm one of them."

"If I lived around here, I'd be one, too. I used to race a bit in my youth, but flying has always been my passion. Why did you stop racing?" Horace asked.

"I stopped after Michael drowned. We argued the night before he died—"

Like you argued with Jonny the night before he died, thought Marjorie.

"There was a rowing practice. Michael turned up drunk and I told him it wasn't safe for him to be out on the water. I was right – the way he was behaving, he could have capsized the boat." Reginald's eyes gazed into the distance.

"I take it he didn't like that?" Horace said.

Reginald shook his head. "He was livid. It was about a week before the regatta. He told me I'd regret it and stormed off in a huff. I should have gone after him but he'd upset Sylvia earlier in the day."

"You mentioned Jonny had upset this woman named Sylvia earlier," said Marjorie. "Who is she?"

"Sylvia Swann was a sports journalist back then and still provides a bit of background for the regatta on a local radio station."

"So, you're suggesting both Michael and Jonny upset this woman shortly before they died?" Horace said.

"Don't go there. Sylvia was devastated when Michael died." He lowered his voice, "They'd been having an affair. It was well known around Henley that Michael wasn't the faithful type."

Marjorie made a mental note about the confirmed relationship between Michael and Sylvia. "Is she the lady who wears a pink suit?"

Reginald stiffened. "No. Why are you asking about Iris?"

"We've noticed her flitting around," said Horace. "I could imagine her being a pundit."

Relaxing again, Reginald took another drink. His glass was almost empty and Marjorie imagined they wouldn't have much longer to question him.

"You're quite wrong. Iris Flame – some people call her Iris Pink because she always wears pink – is a wealthy widow who has taken a keen interest in the regatta since her husband died. He supported the regatta in many ways and came every year. Locals now rely on her donations to teams and other good causes. She likes to make sure the volunteers are happy, even though she's not officially involved."

"Would Jonny have known her before he volunteered?"

"I guess so. Her husband was very well known."

Horace's brow furrowed. "And Michael. Would he have known Iris Flame?"

"Maybe. Now I think about it, Michael had taken a keen interest in Iris's husband for a few months before he drowned."

"Why?"

"It's twenty years ago. I don't remember."

"Would Michael's wife have known about Sylvia Swann?" Marjorie asked.

"Probably. Theirs was a marriage of convenience. They both played away from home, if you know what I mean? No sooner had he died than she married her longtime lover."

"I see," said Marjorie.

"Look, if you want my honest opinion, I believe Michael took his own life. He was a sensitive soul who changed. Like Jonny, he hadn't been right for months before he died. And just like Jonny, he drank too much and was upsetting people."

"Perhaps he was more concerned about his wife's affair than she was about his," said Horace.

"No. He didn't care about that."

"Did anything else happen that might have caused him to change?"

Reginald scrunched his eyes. "Nothing I can think of. Unless—"

"Unless what?" Marjorie asked, watching Reginald's cat-green eyes as they widened in what appeared to be a lightbulb moment.

"Nothing. He was maybe pushing himself too hard or being pushed by his desire to be the best at everything he did. Or maybe someone else was pushing him, I don't know. Something else happened eighteen months before Michael died, but I doubt it had anything to do with the way he changed."

"Tell us anyway," said Horace.

"Michael owned and ran a pharmaceutical research company set up by his father-in-law, and he was managing director initially – that's how he met his wife. He took over the company when his father-in-law retired and employed an old friend from university as the pharmaceutical lead. Casper – the friend – died in a hit-and-run accident walking home after working late one night. Michael was upset about it, obviously, but he worked night and day to keep that business growing. He seemed to get over it pretty quickly."

"Did the police ever find out who ran his friend over?" Marjorie asked.

"I don't think so. It was big news for a few weeks in the local press and then it died down. Michael seemed detached when the police decided it was an open but inactive case."

"Could the driver have been a local?" Marjorie's brain was working overtime, trying to piece together Michael Sebastian's fractured past.

"More likely someone passing through. We used to get yobs over from Reading having a night out. It was generally assumed some teenager had got drunk and knocked the poor guy over. The police interviewed a lot of locals but concluded that whoever did it might not have even known what they'd done. That road was always pitch black at night and it happened in the winter." Reginald had now finished his drink and was back in the present. "I'd better go. But if you want my advice, tell your friend to drop it. There's nothing fishy going on."

Reginald's posture as he walked away suggested he might not be convinced by his own argument.

"What do you think, Marjorie?"

"I'm not sure what to think except I'm more convinced than ever that Frederick's intuition about his friend is correct."

"So, is this about a jealous love triangle twenty years ago, or something else?"

Marjorie considered what Reginald had told them. "We know Jonny was investigating Michael's death. Now we discover Michael had also changed prior to his demise. What we don't know is why. Reginald implied someone was pushing him hard and that he was a sensitive soul. The only major event that might have sparked this change appears to have occurred sometime before."

"Could it have been a delayed reaction?"

"Perhaps. Or he may have stumbled across information that made him believe the person who killed his friend was closer to home than he had initially imagined."

"That's a good point, Marjorie, but I'd be more inclined to believe it had something to do with Michael's chequered history with women or his driven nature."

"Yes, work pressure couldn't have been helped by his heavy drinking. You know how business meetings were always accompanied by too much alcohol in years gone by. And we now know that Medionix Innovations was a pharmaceutical company. Could drugs be involved?"

Horace nodded. "We've got two men with drink problems who had a lot of stress in their lives. It might be the curse in the genes Edna implied causing them to end it all."

"We need to speak to Sylvia Swann. You said she was upset when you saw her inside St Mary's. Michael might have told her what was troubling him and now it's troubling her."

Horace had hardly touched his beer. "Or she might be grieving all over again. Isn't that what we do when we hear about a death similar to that of those closest to us? I know I do."

Marjorie didn't want to rake up her own grief until this case was solved. "Perhaps. Shall we find the others?"

FOURTEEN

Edna had been observing Sir Andrew Eccles for a quarter of an hour, debating within herself what her strategy should be. The guy was seventy-seven, so following Horace's suggestion to do a little flirting wouldn't be outrageous, but she didn't think she'd be able to pull it off. It hadn't taken many minutes to work out she didn't appreciate the way he treated people. With his superior air and dismissive attitude, he just wasn't her type. She would do it her way.

Decision made, Edna sashayed to where he was standing next to a couple who were talking to him, but appeared not to be taking his undisguised disinterest as a hint.

"Excuse me. You look as though you belong here and have some authority. Can you tell me who is responsible for the beehives over there?" Edna pointed in the general direction of the area she was referring to.

"Excuse me while I help this lady," said Sir Andrew, blanking the couple with his back.

Edna grinned. She had been right, he found them boring.

He waggled his eyebrows suggestively. "Why do you want to know?"

"Because they're too close to the public... or should I say, they came too close to me."

His lips curled upwards in a smarmy grin. "Bees like primrose."

Edna chortled. "If they took me for a flower, they weren't thinking straight."

"As much as we need our honeybees, I don't believe they are known for their intelligence. Loyalty to their queen... yes... a bit like we were before our late queen died... but brainpower... I don't think so."

Despite the bombastic nature her friends had mentioned and which she had observed herself, Edna was finding his sense of humour on a par with hers. "At least they're not robotic like wasps."

"Now you have me. I know nothing about wasps. And the primrose yellow suits you, by the way. Would you allow me to buy you a drink? I'm just winding up for the day, and a few people are being a bit too clingy."

Edna looked over his shoulder to see the couple, not easily deterred, still hovering in the background.

"Why not?" she replied, thinking perhaps Horace's suggestion of flirting hadn't been too far off the mark after all.

"Don't tell me. A woman of your sophistication must enjoy a glass of champagne?"

Thankfully, Edna's head had cleared from the effects of the glass she had drunk with lunch. "Champagne will do nicely."

"This way." Sir Andrew motioned with his arm towards the Fawley Bar and, much to the dismay of the hovering couple, they left.

"I don't think your friends were impressed at you leaving them like that," she said.

"I'm sure they'll get over it. Now, Mrs?"

"Edna. Edna Parkinton, I'm a widow."

"Sorry to hear that," he said, the gleam in his eye suggesting otherwise. "Let me get us some champagne and then you can tell me all about your bee encounter."

Edna watched how people kowtowed to the arrogant man, some stepping aside to let him through, and some outwardly deferential.

"Idiots," murmured Edna, "he's just a geezer with money and a title." Horace had money and admittedly, he was a flirt, but he was never superior. Marge had money and a title, just like Sir Andrew Hoity-Toity, but she treated everyone she met with respect. This man used his wealth, title and power to lord it over people.

"Here you are, Edna. I took the liberty of ordering pink champagne."

Arrogance of the man, thought Edna who had expected white. Not that she didn't like pink, but it hadn't taken long to work out that Sir Andrew was a man who did as he pleased and got what he wanted. But was he a murderer? That's what she was here to find out.

"Thank you. But you have the advantage of me."

"How's that?"

"I don't know your name." A little white lie never hurt.

"Sir Andrew Eccles at your service."

And there it was. Marjorie rarely introduced herself with her title unless she needed to for investigative purposes. "*Sir* Andrew?"

"But you may call me Andrew."

"Were you born a sir?" She already knew the answer and would have loved to add, 'or did you buy it?' But that would have antagonised him.

"It came as a reward for my charitable works."

Edna raised her glass and sipped the champagne. "Mm." The taste suited her palate and she couldn't help enjoying it.

"Good, isn't it? I recognise a woman who appreciates the finer things in life when I see one."

And I recognise a man who's full of... went unsaid. "About those beehives?"

"And I thought that was a chat-up line," he said, winking.

"They really did come after me, but no harm was done so I'm happy to flatter your ego. Tell me about yourself."

"Like am I married?" He really was full of himself.

"If you're going to pretend you're not, you should spray-tan the ring finger after you remove the ring."

"Ouch. Intelligent as well as pretty."

"Seriously, tell me about yourself. What's your involvement in the regatta?"

"How do you know I have any involvement?"

"It's something about the way people treat you. Is it one of your charitable works?"

"Okay, I'm sort of involved in that I come every year. I help make sure things run smoothly but in an informal capacity."

Like making sure bodies are removed quickly. "Well, you're doing a good job. I'm having a great time."

"Apart from the bees."

"Yes. Apart from the bees. You should speak to someone about getting those hives moved."

"Consider it done." Sir Andrew gave her an appraising look. "Are you alone at the regatta?"

"I came with friends, but we do our own thing. You were telling me about yourself."

"Boats are my business. I wouldn't want to bore you with the details but I have a boatyard in Norfolk and sell boats all around the country."

"Not the world?"

"I still sell to Europe, although it isn't easy since Brexit. Having said that, I'm less and less involved in the business these days. My nephew runs it. He'll inherit when I'm gone, so I wanted to see if he could make a go of it. He's been a good choice as it happens and is making it more successful every day."

"Do you have children?"

"Three. Two daughters, a son and a handful of grandkids."

He might have been talking about commodities for all the feeling that *didn't* go into that sentence.

"You?"

"Sadly no. We wanted children, but it never happened."

"Mine have gone their own way. I can't say I mind; I travel a lot. My nephew understands the business. Were you a lady of leisure or did you work yourself, Edna?"

"I was a singer. Nothing famous, like, but I made a decent living out of it."

"There doesn't seem to be an end to your talents. What else are you hiding?"

"I would imagine that as well as pretending not to be married, it would be you who has things to hide, Sir Andrew."

His face suddenly turned puce. "Who sent you?"

"Pardon?"

"What do they want?"

"Hey, calm down. It was a joke."

He forced a chuckle. "Of course."

"Are you okay?"

"Yes, I'm fine. I thought for a moment, you might be one of those people sent by some charity to worm your way into my wallet."

That reaction had been nothing to do with charities: he was hiding something. "This really is great champagne," she said, taking another sip and waiting for him to relax. "You come here every year, then? Don't you get bored?"

"If I'm honest, it's a place where a lot of business deals are done."

"That makes more sense," said Edna. "I'm enjoying the racing but it wouldn't be a regular on my itinerary."

"If you look beneath the surface, Edna, you will discover that it's a community within a community. Look beyond the superficial, you'll find everything good about human endeavour. Hard work, discipline, dedication and artistry."

"Not to mention boozing, affairs, dishonesty and probably even murder," she said.

"I didn't have you down as a cynic."

"And I didn't have you down as a person who looked at life through rose-tinted spectacles," Edna retorted.

"I like your straight talking but be careful what you say around here. People take things personally."

"So I gather," said Edna.

"You didn't bump into me by chance, did you?" Andrew sighed, and she almost felt sorry for him. "What do you want?"

"Why don't you get me another one of these and I'll tell you?"

Andrew left, and then returned to the table with two glasses of pink champagne, wedding ring back where it should be. Edna grinned.

"Sorry for being presumptuous," he said.

"And I'm sorry for misleading you."

He took out his cheque book. "Because you had me, you deserve a donation. What's the charity?"

"No charity. I wanted to ask you why you chivvied the police along yesterday morning, when Jonny Sebastian was found drowned, and how come you found one body twenty years ago and were in the vicinity where another was discovered?"

"Horace Tyler is one of the friends you're with?"

Edna smiled. "I'd also like to know why you objected to Jonny Sebastian volunteering at the regatta. Take your time."

"Okay, Edna. Because I like you – a lot more than Horace, by the way – I'll humour you. Getting the body moved should be obvious. There's a famous regatta going on and as the police found no reason to suspect the death was anything other than an accident, I pushed to have it moved."

"Fair enough," said Edna. "But how come your shoes were muddy and your trousers wet?"

"How on earth? Don't tell me – the sharp-eyed friend who caught my distaste for Jonny Sebastian?"

Edna grinned once more. "Her name is Marjorie Snellthorpe... *Lady* Marjorie Snellthorpe."

"Touché. I'm sorry to disappoint, but rather than drowning an unpleasant man, I had stepped out of the way of a huge beast of a Saint Bernard and landed in a deep puddle. There was a lot of rain a few weeks ago and the remnants remain on that side of the bridge. It doesn't get as much sun."

Edna chortled. "I'd have paid money to see that."

Andrew's eyes crinkled into a grin. "Needless to say, I changed afterwards."

Edna had already checked his pristine flannel trousers and shiny brown leather shoes. "I wouldn't have expected otherwise."

"As for finding the other body you mentioned, I suppose you're referring to that of Michael Sebastian. It so happened I was in Henley for business meetings prior to the event that year. We were selling about twenty boats to various entities. One of my meetings was to be with Michael. He owned a company that employed nurses, a pharmacist and scientists to carry out research for the bigger pharmaceutical companies. The arrangement meant the larger conglomerates didn't need to employ the staff directly. Michael was about to buy a boat for his team. Businesses, as well as schools, colleges and professionals, take part in the regatta and as Michael was a rower himself, he wanted to get his employees involved."

"Anything else?"

"As I told Horace, he also had a reputation as a womaniser."

Edna raised an eyebrow and Andrew lifted a hand.

"I know, I know. I've got no room to talk, but he was far less subtle."

"You mean he didn't remove his wedding ring."

"No. I mean he went from one relationship to another, rubbing his wife's face in it because she was having an affair. It was as if he was jealous, which seemed ludicrous."

"He wouldn't be the first man to want his own pizza and scoff someone else's."

"Nice saying. On the day he died, we had arranged to meet by Henley Bridge and then walk to my place. I have a house by the river on the Oxfordshire side and had a converted office in the garden. When I arrived, I saw someone floating in the Thames. I didn't know who it was at first, so I waded out. When I turned him over, I couldn't believe my eyes. I called Elsa."

"Who's Elsa and why didn't you call for an ambulance?"

"I was in shock, but even so, it was clear the body had been in the water for some hours. Elsa Christie was a local GP and the regatta doctor and could get there faster than any ambulance. When she arrived, she told me to go home while she called the police."

"Why the police?"

"Apparently, it's routine for unexpected deaths. An inquest confirmed death by drowning. There were high levels of alcohol in his blood and his rowing mates confirmed he'd been drunk the night before, so the coroner concluded death by misadventure."

"I'm reliably informed Jonny Sebastian was a strong swimmer; do you know if his cousin swam?"

"We weren't on friendship terms but most rowers are excellent swimmers. They have to be."

"You didn't think it suspicious that he drowned?"

"I had a lot of hats to juggle back then, Edna, and this might sound callous, but I didn't care enough about the man to give it much thought. If anything, I was annoyed at losing the sale. I'd gone to a lot of trouble and expense to get him the right boat. Regarding Jonny Sebastian's arrival in Henley, I heard he'd been throwing accusations around, some of which were aimed at me. That's why I didn't like the fact he was volunteering at the regatta."

"Right."

"I'm not saying there's nothing to investigate. Two deaths like that in the same place would raise anyone's eyebrows, but just like yesterday, the police found nothing suspicious. Let me make one thing clear though, Edna. Neither death had anything to do with me."

FIFTEEN

"Excuse me? Where can I find Dr Elsa Christie?" Frederick had waited until the first aid tent was empty before asking a St John Ambulance volunteer.

"Dr Christie hasn't worked at the regatta for years."

"I was told she sometimes hangs out near here," Frederick persisted.

"Hang on a minute." The man poked his head inside the tent. "Has anyone seen Elsa Christie today?"

"No, but she'll be in the smoking zone south of here," a woman replied.

The man pointed to Frederick's left. "The smoking area's over there."

"How will I recognise her?" Frederick asked.

"Just ask anyone wearing a member's badge. If she's there, they'll point her out to you."

After a few minutes' walking, Frederick saw the designated smoking sign. He entered the enclosure and immediately felt irritation at the back of his throat. Childhood asthma had left him with a weakness. He always found cigarette smoke robbed him of his breath, which, in part, was psychological.

Calm down, Mackworth, he told himself. *You're outdoors. There's plenty of fresh air to breathe.*

He stepped cautiously into a refreshment tent and asked a bartender if he had seen the doctor. "She's got her own deckchair with her name on the back. Usually parks it near the river on the left-hand side next to the fence to annoy the non-smokers on the other side. Elsa's not one for rules."

"Thank you," said Frederick, feeling more confident about finding his target, but much less so about approaching her.

"Go easy, she's in a mood."

"Oh?" With his final shred of confidence ebbing away, Frederick debated whether to give up on his task. He had wasted a lot of time trying to track her down and the thought of speaking to a stranger in a bad mood had little appeal. It was imagining Edna's derision that drove him on.

The hand-painted name on the back of the deckchair made it unmissable. Dr Christie was exactly where the bartender had told him she would be. Smoke wafted his way, carried on the breeze. Resisting the urge to cough, he dodged a large plume, accidentally bumping into a man heading for the river.

"Sorry."

The man ignored him and weaved his way through others looking for seats. He was clearly determined to get near the river front and wasn't stopping for conversation. Frederick took a small step forward, trying to appear casual, until he was standing next to the solitary deckchair. The placement of the chair, together with Dr Christie's body language, couldn't have been clearer if she'd had a Stay Away warning sign painted on the rear alongside her name. But if she wanted to be left alone, why put her name on the chair in the first place?

Feeling slightly awkward standing where he was between the neatly laid-out deckchairs on his right and Dr Christie's lone one to his left, he plucked up courage to say something. He opened his mouth to speak, but clamped it shut again when she removed another cigarette from a silver case and lit it with the one she had just finished.

A chain smoker.

"Talk about stating the bloomin' obvious." He heard Edna's voice booming in his head, which made him splutter a sound between a laugh and a cough.

Dr Christie cast a sharp sideways glance in his direction. She appeared to be in her late sixties with dyed brown hair tied in a bun, which made her look even harsher than he had been told she was. Her green eyes were cat-like and he felt every bit the prey standing there.

"Sorry," he said. "I was thinking of a friend."

"Don't mind me. You know you're not allowed to stand, don't you?"

"I forgot," he said, remembering how Horace had supplied the dos and don'ts of expected behaviour inside the Stewards' Enclosure.

"That one's empty," she motioned to a chair on the end of a row on the right. Vacant, no doubt, because she had driven the poor occupant away with her vibes.

"Thanks." Grimacing and waiting for her to protest, he pulled the chair across and placed it next to hers.

"Do I know you?" she asked, blowing smoke in his face.

"No," said Frederick, unable to stifle a cough, "but if you are Doctor Elsa Christie, I think you knew an old friend of mine. My name's Frederick, Frederick Mackworth."

"Who's the old friend?"

Plucking up every ounce of courage he had, and channelling his inner superhero, he mumbled, "Jonny Sebastian."

Dr Christie stopped puffing on her cigarette as her lips tightened into a fine line. Recovering, she took the next drag, deliberately blowing smoke in his direction again. The nicotine staining to the fingers of her right hand wasn't as marked as he would expect from someone dragging on the item in it as if her life depended on it. He guessed she once used a cigarette holder.

"Henley's a small town and I used to be a GP; I knew his parents more than him. He moved back recently, I heard."

"My late wife was a doctor and knew every patient on her list. Things are different now; I rarely get to see the same GP twice, and they wouldn't know me if I passed them in the street. I expect you're glad to be retired," he said.

"For so many reasons," Dr Christie appeared to relax, blowing her smoke away from him this time. "As you say, it's a different health service now. Gone are the days when the patient–doctor relationship was like that of a priest and a member of his congregation. Even I struggle to get an appointment if I need one. Were you a doctor?"

"I was a pharmacist."

Dr Christie smiled. "They're not the same anymore either. Some of them have the same attitude as the modern doctor. It's all about money these days. We used to have a good relationship with our local pharmacist, but now the shop's been taken over by the big boys."

Bitter she may be, but at least she was opening up. Frederick kept up the friendly chit-chat.

"My kids didn't want to pursue either profession, and I can't blame them."

"My son's the same. He's an Oxford graduate."

"What does he do?" Frederick asked.

Dr Christie's eyes glazed over. "He, erm... It's difficult to explain."

Frederick got the impression this part of the conversation was over, so he took a deep breath before saying, "Did you know Jonny was found drowned yesterday morning?"

"What?" Frederick's words appeared to break the spell of the doctor's ruminating as she looked at him. "No, I didn't hear that." She broke eye contact and stared out at the water.

"I ran into him on the first day of the regatta after not seeing him for years. He was a fellow pharmacist, but I expect you know that. We went for a drink and he seemed upset. I think it had something to do with his cousin Michael. I take it you knew Michael from your GP days?" Frederick was blurting out the words due to his nervousness.

"Yes, I knew Michael Sebastian. He ran a pharmaceutical research business on the Reading Road, Medionix Innovations. He was also an amateur rower. Our paths crossed in both spheres but mostly in relation to his company. My practice participated in some of the trials they were paid to run and I gave my time to the regatta as a medic. He drowned as well, but I'm assuming you know that. A man called Andrew Eccles – he's Sir Andrew now, but he wasn't back then – called me after he found Michael's body in the river."

"Is that unusual? I would have thought it best to call an ambulance."

"He panicked and knew I was just up the road. Besides, when I got there, Michael had been in the water for far too long for anyone to have made a difference. I confirmed death and called the police.

"There was an inquest, of course, and the verdict was death by misadventure. I believe alcohol had a part to play. The pathologist found high blood-alcohol levels which, I don't need to tell you, would have impaired his judgement. His wife testified at the inquest that when he was feeling low, he went late-night swimming."

"Did Jonny ask you about Michael's death?"

"A week ago. For some reason, he thought someone else might have been responsible, but I can assure you, there was no evidence of that. I told him as much."

"Was suicide ever considered?"

"It was mentioned and dismissed. Michael suffered mood

swings, but he was also driven. Not the kind of man in my experience to take his own life."

"What about Jonny?"

"Are you asking whether I believe Jonny Sebastian could have committed suicide? I didn't know him well enough to give an opinion. What I gather is that he was bereft enough following his wife's death to come back to Henley on some sort of witch hunt over something that was an open-and-shut case. You mentioned he was troubled when you saw him, did he tell you why?"

Frederick wondered whether to confide in Dr Christie who, he was pleased to see, had stubbed out the latest cigarette without lighting another, but Marjorie wouldn't approve. "I asked, but he wouldn't say. I got a text in the middle of the night asking me to meet him early yesterday morning. I didn't get the message until the meeting time had passed and by the time I got to the river, the police were pulling his body out of the water." Frederick felt his voice cracking and paused before adding, "That Sir Andrew you mentioned was there, hurrying the police and paramedics out of the vicinity."

"Oh dear. You must feel awful."

Frederick dropped his head. "I wish he'd told me what was troubling him."

"Did the police say anything?"

"They didn't find anything suspicious. They interviewed me later but were looking at accident or suicide. I was wondering if you would speak to the pathologist and find out what they discover. The police said there would be a post-mortem today."

"Why me?"

"Because they're more likely to speak to you than to me. I don't think Jonny would have killed himself, but, like his cousin Michael, he'd been drinking heavily."

"This is sounding like a familiar story," said Dr Christie. "Are you prepared for the outcome if the police find a note?"

"They won't."

"What makes you so sure?"

Frederick had slipped up and he knew it. He thought fast. "We go back a long way, and Jonny was a fighter. He seemed resigned to the fact Judith had died and told me he had something important to do before selling his parents' home. That doesn't sound like someone about to kill himself, does it?"

"No, it doesn't. There are no guarantees, but I can make a few telephone calls and ask who did the post-mortem. If it's someone I know, I'll see what I can find out."

"Would you? I'd be really grateful."

"You've had a shock, it's the least I can do. Are you staying in Henley for long?"

"Until the end of the regatta. We're at Dinah's Hotel."

"We?"

"Yes. I'm here with friends. Horace Tyler is Dinah's grandfather and a member here."

"I don't remember a Horace Tyler."

"He used to bring people on hospitality days. Horace owns an avionics firm but his sons run it now. He hasn't been to the regatta for years, although he used to row."

Dr Christie's brow furrowed. "Obviously our paths didn't cross. I was often stuck in the first aid tent during the regatta and since retiring a few years ago, I've taken a back seat."

"Believe me, if you'd met Horace, you would remember him."

"Oh?"

Frederick felt he was being disloyal. "We're complete opposites: he's outgoing and I'm... more introspective. He knows Sir Andrew, or at least they did business together some time way back."

Dr Christie removed another cigarette from the case as the

noise levels rose, signalling a race was coming closer. Frederick tore a page out of the tiny notebook he always carried and scribbled his number down.

"Please let me know if you manage to find out anything about Jonny's death."

Dr Christie lit up before taking the piece of paper and placing it in her handbag. "No promises, you understand?"

"I do, but anything you can find out will be appreciated. I'm hoping his daughter will travel up from Cornwall, and I'll have a word with her when she arrives."

"Tread carefully, Frederick. People who have lost a loved one can be sensitive."

"You're right. I'll wait until I hear from you." Frederick had hoped for an exchange of telephone numbers, but Dr Christie showed no inclination of giving him one. Her attention was now on the water... and her cigarette.

"Put that chair back where you found it, would you?"

Frederick did as commanded. He'd done well to get her to talk at all considering her demeanour when he arrived. Even Edna would be proud of how much he'd managed to find out. The only thing he'd forgotten to ask about was Michael's girlfriend, but he doubted they would have been close enough for her to know anything other than hearsay.

SIXTEEN

Back at Dinah's after eating a delicious pub dinner on the outskirts of Henley, the four friends retreated into the closed bar in the hotel. The pub where they had enjoyed their meal had been too busy to have a private conversation without risk of being overheard.

"Would any of you like a nightcap?" Horace asked.

Edna's eyes lit up. "I wouldn't say no to a whisky."

"Let's not disturb Dinah, it's late," said Marjorie.

"It's all right, she said we could help ourselves," said Horace. "I'll pay her in the morning."

"Well in that case, I'd love a brandy."

"What about you, Fred?"

"The same as Marjorie please."

The contemporary bar was interesting to study while Horace poured their drinks. If she'd been in charge of the interior design, Dinah showed good taste. She had managed to sympathetically meld original features with modern, an achievement that wasn't easy without creating a mess. Light grey walls added warmth to the large and high-ceilinged room.

The old chandelier had been converted to allow for LED lighting.

"Practical as well as modern," murmured Marjorie.

"Pardon?" said Horace as he placed two large glasses of whisky on the table for himself and Edna, and smaller helpings of brandy for Marjorie and Frederick. He knew them well.

"Did I say that out loud? I was admiring your granddaughter's eye for detail and the use of LED bulbs. With such a high ceiling, having the lighting adapted means no-one has to climb a large ladder on a regular basis to change them. I had spotlights installed in my kitchen recently and the electrician insisted on fitting LED, assuring me they will last for years."

Edna blew out an impatient breath. "I can't believe you're discussing interior design, Marge, when I'm dying to tell you about my conversation with Horace's mate, Andrew."

"I'm listening," said Marjorie.

"I didn't go for the flirty approach, I decided to ask him who was responsible for placing the beehives so close to the public areas."

Ignoring an exasperated sigh from Frederick, Edna continued. "He's a one, that Sir Andy. As soon as we got talking, he took his wedding ring off as if his luck was in. I soon put him straight."

"I bet that went down well," said Frederick.

"He didn't mind actually," said Edna. "Men like him are chancers, but he took it all in his stride. It turned out I ran into him at the right time, he was being bored stiff by a couple who couldn't take a hint. We had pink champagne."

"I thought you seemed a bit flushed when you got back, and wondered why you declined wine in the pub. There I was thinking you might have fallen for Andrew's charm, it got me right here." Horace placed a hand on his heart.

"Stop messing, Horace Tyler. By the way, I don't think he

likes you any more than you like him. He said he'd much rather speak to a pretty woman than you."

"Never was a man more misunderstood," said Horace.

"Yeah, so you've said a thousand times."

"As entertaining as this banter is, it's getting late, and as you made a point of doing away with small talk, Edna, I'd like to keep on track," said Marjorie.

"All right, Marge, keep your hair on!"

Marjorie resisted the temptation to point out that it wasn't her wearing a wig, but she'd done that once before. It had been cruel then, and it would be worse if she did it again. As annoying as Edna and her sayings could be at times, it wasn't her fault she suffered from permanent alopecia.

"I got Sir Andy Flirty-Gertie to admit to being annoyed when he saw Jonny volunteering."

"He blatantly denied it when I asked him," said Horace.

"As I said, he liked me." Edna held a hand up to Marjorie who was about to ask her again to keep to the point. "Okay, okay. He told me he was annoyed because Jonny had been going about stirring up trouble and throwing accusations around to do with his cousin Michael's death."

"Who did he throw accusations at?" Frederick asked.

"Sir Andrew, for one," said Edna. "I hate to disappoint you, Marge, but it's neither a surprise nor suspicious that he was down near the river yesterday morning. He owns a house not far from where Jonny was found. Sorry, Fred, I don't think he had anything to do with either his or Michael's death."

"Oh, he really did charm you," said Horace.

Edna gave a sly grin. "Jealousy will get you nowhere."

"Did you ask him about his shoes and trousers?" Marjorie asked.

"Yes. Apparently, he was avoiding a large dog that was taking no prisoners. A Saint Burmese or something..."

"A Saint Bernard or a Burmese, there's no such thing as a Saint Burmese," said Frederick.

"Oh, you're a dog expert now as well as a drugs encyclopaedia, are you? Anyway, to avoid the *Saint Bernard*, he accidentally stepped into a deep puddle. He also had a good reason for finding Michael Sebastian's body when he died. They had arranged to meet that morning because Michael was buying a boat for some sort of team building exercise. Apparently, he owned a research place."

"Dr Christie mentioned the research company too," said Frederick.

"As did Reginald," said Horace. "He also confirmed Michael's lover at the time of his death was Sylvia Swann. I looked up Medionix Innovations. They went into voluntary insolvency a decade ago. The listing at Companies House shows them as dissolved. Michael was a director, as was his wife, but she resigned about six months after his death. The offices were out on the A4155, which explains how easy it would have been for a hit-and-run to happen twenty-odd years ago. I used to drive along that road sometimes. It's dark and bendy and this was long before the days of CCTV."

"What's a hit-and-run got to do with anything?" Frederick's forehead creased.

"When Horace and I spoke to Reginald," replied Marjorie, "he remembered one of Michael's friends, someone he employed as his pharmaceutical lead, being killed in a hit-and-run accident about eighteen months prior to Michael's death. He also hinted that Michael was pushing himself, or being pushed too hard. I wonder if Michael internalised his friend Casper's death at the time and it later affected his behaviour."

"He was juggling a complicated social life which might have had an effect on the latter. The hit-and-run is unlikely to have any bearing on either his or Jonny's death. But I'm just saying the A roads can be dangerous if you don't drive sensibly... What's the matter, Edna?"

Marjorie followed Horace's eyes. Edna was fidgeting in her chair.

"The hit-and-run *could* have something to do with our case," she said.

Horace looked confused. "Why? Did Andrew mention it?"

"No. It was the newspapers."

Frederick shook his head. "I'm not following, what newspapers?"

"When I was looking for stuff about Michael. I didn't think it was relevant."

"Edna, you're not making sense," said Horace.

"At Jonny's house, along with stories about Michael, there was a separate pile of local newspapers covering a hit-and-run. Casper Wolff, the man's name was – I remember because it was an odd one. The articles were appealing for witnesses. Sorry, I just didn't join the dots."

"Why would you," said Horace, "without the full picture?"

Marjorie felt a satisfying warmth at the back of her throat as the brandy went down. "You know what, Edna? You may have found the missing link."

"Really?" Edna's face shone.

"I don't get it," said Frederick.

"I'm not sure I do either," Marjorie admitted, "but we know Jonny was looking into his cousin Michael's death."

"Which Dr Christie and the subsequent inquest say wasn't suspicious," said Frederick.

"It wouldn't seem to be at first glance. Michael had a drink problem and had been drinking heavily the night before his death. We can assume he didn't commit suicide because he wouldn't have arranged to meet Sir Andrew to buy a boat for his company if that had been his intention."

"That's what Andrew said," Edna added.

"But what if, as Jonny's research suggests, Michael had stumbled upon the person who drove the vehicle that killed his friend, Casper? Imagine Michael confronting this person, or persons, who had managed to avoid detection, and them having no intention of being found out."

"Because they were a pillar of society," added Horace.

"We can't be certain of that, but Jonny seemed to be leaning that way, with Sir Andrew being one of those in his sights."

Frederick rubbed his head. "So, you're suggesting Jonny might have also discovered who this driver was and put the pieces together, and that's what got him killed?"

"It's a possibility," said Marjorie.

"As much as I like being credited with finding a missing link, Marge, it all seems too far-fetched. If you're right, we've got someone running around Henley killing people to cover up a crime that happened over twenty years ago."

"Marjorie's theory makes sense," said Horace. "Other than a jealous husband or Michael's widow—"

"Who lives abroad and hasn't returned to Henley in years," said Frederick. "I looked her up."

"Right. So, other than a jealous husband, and we've discounted suicide, whoever killed the two men might be somebody willing to use drastic measures to protect their secret."

"But the newspaper article suggested the car was driven by an out-of-towner."

"An excuse to drop the case," said Marjorie.

"Or a deliberate diversion from someone with influence," added Horace.

Edna puffed out her cheeks before blowing out the stored air. "I still say we're missing the facts. As sad as it is that two men are dead, both of them were heavy drinkers and both could have fallen into the river and drowned while under the influence. That's what Andrew thinks happened, although he acknowledged it's an odd coincidence now Jonny is dead."

"Well, he would say that, wouldn't he?" Frederick snapped. "Who's to say he didn't do it? And after finding Michael, why did he call Dr Christie, a woman he knew, rather than the police or paramedics?"

"I presume Dr Christie told you that?" Edna asked.

"Yes, she said he was in shock. It was her who called the police."

"Yeah, but he admitted that to me. He said it was obvious the bloke was dead and when Dr Christie got there, she told him to go home. It can't have been nice for him."

"He's really got you believing him, hasn't he?" Frederick retorted.

"As Marge said earlier, it's not usually the killer who reports finding the body."

"Unless they're going in for major misdirection," said Frederick. "I've watched a few documentaries where killers do exactly that. Sorry, Marjorie."

"I don't claim to be an expert on these things," said Marjorie, although in this case, she didn't believe Sir Andrew would have sufficient motive. "Perhaps we should find out whether Sir Andrew was in Henley in the days before or after the hit-and-run incident."

"We should speak to the journalist who covered that story in case he was," said Frederick. "Dr Christie agreed to speak to the pathologist if she can. I gave her my phone number in case."

"Along with everyone else. You've been dishing out your card like smarties," said Edna.

"Someone might remember something," said Frederick, defensively.

"What's Dr Christie like?" Horace asked. "I never met her, but I've been thinking back and I believe she had a bit of a reputation."

"What sort of reputation?" Edna asked. "Don't tell me she was involved in doping."

"Nothing like that. I think people were afraid of her."

"She's prickly, that's for sure; a rough diamond, I'd say," said Frederick. "But, apart from being a chain smoker and a bit stand-offish, she seems okay. I was warned before I met her that she was in a mood."

"Trust you to wheedle your way in," said Edna, "but well done at the same time."

Frederick's bald head flushed at the compliment. "Thank you. We found some common ground. Oh, and she says she knew Michael from his rowing and his work with the research company. Her practice took part in some of the trials."

Marjorie was trying to piece together everything they knew. "That's interesting. What were her thoughts regarding his death?"

"Same as the others. She said his blood alcohol levels were raised and the police didn't find any evidence of anything other than death by misadventure. We... or I... could be barking up the wrong tree."

Marjorie cupped her chin in her hand. "I don't think so, but if these men were murdered for whatever reason – and I'm leaning towards the hit-and-run – we are looking for a ruthless killer who won't hesitate to kill again. We should be careful while shaking any more branches."

"It might be a bit late for that," said Horace.

"What next then, Marge?"

"As well as researching the past, there are a few more people to speak to: Sylvia Swann, and Iris Flame, the lady in pink."

"Not to mention the police," suggested Edna. "We should tell them what we've found out so far."

"I'd say we postpone that until we've got something that doesn't suggest we are a quartet of busybodies who don't have anything better to do with our time than conjure up murder theories," said Marjorie. "Any detective worth their salt will have found Jonny's research when going through his house and should be following up any leads."

"Fred can do the research into the death of Casper Wolff and see what drugs the company was researching at the time," Horace said. "During the regatta tomorrow, we'll see who else we can speak to. We haven't tried Oswald Greene on his own yet."

"Fine. But for now, I'm going to bed, I'm bushed," said Edna.

"Me too," said Frederick.

"We'll just finish our nightcaps. Another, Marjorie?" Horace's tone suggested he wanted a private word.

"No, thank you, but I'll stay and finish this one."

Once the others left, Horace said, "If you're right and there is a killer out there, I don't want you or Edna being put at risk."

"You know Edna would call you a dinosaur for saying that, don't you?"

"I can't help who I am. And on the other hand, all we've got so far is hearsay and two dead men with drink problems. Do you really believe we should be pursuing this?"

Marjorie's heart sank at the idea Horace might be losing faith. "We're getting somewhere, and although it's convoluted, I believe we should persevere for Frederick's sake."

"Okay. That's good enough for me. We'll start again tomorrow, as long as we stick together."

Horace drained his glass and bid her goodnight. Marjorie sat in the armchair for a long time after the others had retired, going over all the different scenarios in her head.

SEVENTEEN

The four friends reiterated their next course of action over breakfast. Frederick had already searched the internet and tracked down the journalist who reported on the hit-and-run accident twenty-two years ago, and he seemed happier and more motivated this morning.

"She has retired to Brighton, but as it turns out, she's one of a small number of people still listed in the telephone directory. Her name is Sharon Taylor. I'm going to give her a call later this morning."

"Excellent work, Fred," said Horace.

"I still think Jonny was on a wild goose chase and we're wasting our time," complained Edna, who had been quiet over breakfast. Marjorie wondered if she was finding the long days too much. It wasn't that long since she'd been hospitalised with pneumonia.

Marjorie patted her forearm. "Would you like to stay at the hotel today?"

Horace's brow furrowed, concern in his eyes. "Are you all right, Edna?"

"I'm just a bit tired, that's all. I'll be fine once we get

moving."

Marjorie admired her stoicism. Edna wouldn't want to let them down. *Or miss out on the action*, an inner voice told her.

"If we don't get any real leads today, I think we should go back to enjoying the regatta," said Frederick. "I don't want to waste anyone's time and ruin the few days we have left."

"What do you suggest, Marjorie?" Horace asked.

With all eyes on her, Marjorie felt conflicted. Deep down she believed Frederick's instincts were right, but a part of her brain wanted to capitulate and let it go.

"As Frederick suggests, we'll give it one more day before we leave things alone, except for one thing." She looked at Frederick. "You must update the police."

Frederick nodded.

"We're in agreement then," said Horace. "We'll shake a few more branches and rattle some cages."

"As long as we don't forget I need a new pair of shoes," said Edna.

Frederick's eyebrows almost reached where his hairline would once have been.

"I'll take you at lunchtime, although the ones you're wearing today are very attractive."

Edna grinned. "I brought a few pairs along. A woman can never have too many shoes."

Marjorie couldn't agree less, although when she thought about it, she had in excess of twenty pairs at home, despite wearing the same three pairs most of the time.

Thirty minutes later, the quartet ambled through the now familiar entrance into the Stewards' Enclosure. Marjorie wasn't sure whether the excited anticipation surging through her body was because she was enjoying the races, or whether it was due to being immersed in a complex puzzle. Jonny Sebastian's death had thrown up all sorts of challenges.

The reality was that it was a mixture of the two. Having

agreed to let the whole thing go if they didn't make progress today, she longed to help Frederick find closure. His friend's death had resulted in him going through an emotional rollercoaster which she wanted to assist him to walk away from.

They were no more than a few feet inside the grounds where the early morning crowds were gathering when their attention was drawn to a commotion.

"This is absurd!" A loud voice Marjorie recognised made her turn her head to the right. Sir Andrew's face was no longer just ruddy, it was puce as he yelled at a burly man with thinning blond hair, wearing a tailored brown suit. The man and a younger red-headed woman with him weren't wearing member or guest badges.

"If you'd like to come with us, sir," the man said.

"Why should I? This is ridiculous. Go and bother someone else. I'm needed here."

"It would be better if you came willingly, sir," said the man, stepping closer to Sir Andrew.

"Or what?"

"Or I'm going to have to take you in under caution."

Sir Andrew's mouth opened wide and closed again like a large goldfish gasping for air. He accepted the challenge.

"Fine. Arrest me."

If Sir Andrew had hoped his dismissive tone would work on the detective standing in front of him, his bluff failed.

"If you insist, sir. Sergeant, do the honours, would you."

"Sir Andrew Eccles, I am arresting you on suspicion of the murder of Mr Jonathan Sebastian. You do not have to say anything..."

While the sergeant finished reciting his rights to Sir Andrew, Marjorie noticed Iris Flame a few metres away, trembling, with a distraught look on her face.

"This is ridiculous. You'll be sorry when my lawyer gets to the station."

The senior officer appeared unmoved, almost smug, as he and his sergeant ushered Sir Andrew towards the entrance. As he passed them, Sir Andrew caught Edna's eye and, seeing Horace, he stopped moving, shaking his head.

"It seems you were right; Jonathan Sebastian was murdered and these id—" He refrained from antagonising the arresting officers any further, saying, "... these members of Thames Valley Police think I had something to do with it." He leaned forward and whispered to Horace, "I didn't. And as it looks like these people have already made up their minds, I'm putting my trust in you and your motley crew." At this point, he looked at Marjorie. "Use your sharp observation skills to find out who did it, because it wasn't me."

The sergeant had been listening carefully and opened her mouth as if about to speak to them, but her senior was losing patience.

"Come along, we haven't got all day."

A few people stopped on hearing the commotion, but most of it, apart from Sir Andrew's loud protestations, had gone unnoticed as the buzz of the regatta gradually filled the air. Minutes later, all was normal again, except Frederick had turned pale. Iris Flame, the lady who always seemed to wear pink, was pretending to peer at the river through a long-handled lorgnette.

"What do you say about that, Marge? I could have sworn he was telling the truth yesterday."

Marjorie didn't reply, she was already on her way over to Iris Flame. "Excuse me? I'm so sorry to interrupt, but I believe you and Sir Andrew are friends. We saw what happened just now. Would you mind telling us about it from your perspective?"

Marjorie's three friends arrived at her side. The petite woman regained a little of her composure as she looked at them.

"You must be Jonathan Sebastian's friends. Andrew told me you'd been asking questions."

Following a round of introductions, Iris glared at Frederick.

"Was it you who called the police?"

"He didn't, none of us did," said Marjorie. "We are as surprised by their presence here this morning as you are."

"They're saying Jonny was drugged and held under the water. From the little I heard, the inspector suggested someone murdered him because of something that happened years ago."

"Regarding Michael Sebastian?" said Frederick.

Iris stared at Frederick, still trembling slightly. "Jonny had been making wild accusations that Andrew had killed his cousin twenty years ago. Now the police want to question him about both deaths. But they have no evidence. Andrew's incapable of killing anyone, despite his bluster. Underneath all that he's got a heart of gold."

"How well do you know Sir Andrew?" Marjorie asked.

"We've met at the regatta and on charity committees over the years." Although Iris's face remained blank, the fact she wouldn't meet Marjorie's eyes suggested she knew him better than she was saying.

"Is there any reason why the police believe Andrew responsible, other than him finding Michael's body?" Horace asked.

"I don't think so. There was some gossip after Michael's accident that he had uncovered a betting scandal Andrew was involved in, but it was a rumour with no substance. Andrew doesn't gamble."

"And what about Michael?" Marjorie asked gently. "Was he an honest man?"

"Michael Sebastian was lovely when sober, but when he'd been drinking, he became a different person, stirring up trouble. I didn't know him well, but my husband did. He invested in Michael's father-in-law's business when it was just a startup."

"That's interesting. Did he get a return on his investment?" Horace asked.

"I believe so, but they had a falling out when Michael took over."

"Because of the drinking?" Frederick asked.

"My husband never went into details on business matters, but I think Michael threatened him. But that was all in the past until Jonny Sebastian came back to Henley on some kind of vendetta. He was determined to throw mud at Andrew. Jonny should have just left people to get on with their lives. It's never a good thing to rake up the past." Iris looked through the lorgnette again, feigning disinterest.

"If what you say is true and Sir Andrew is innocent, we'd like to help him," said Marjorie. "Did Jonny accuse anybody else of being involved in his cousin's death?"

"He seemed determined to dig up dirt on anyone who knew Michael."

"Including you?" Edna asked.

"There's nothing to find," Iris replied with a sugar-sweet smile and doe eyes. "Me, I don't believe anybody was murdered. Jonny probably got tired of his toxic game and took the drugs himself. He was bitter enough to have ended his own life to make it look like murder."

"That's quite the accusation," said Frederick. "Jonny was my friend."

"I'm sorry, but he was a pharmacist and very determined. If he couldn't pin his cousin's murder on anyone in life, perhaps he planned to make sure someone was held responsible for his own death. Now, if you'll excuse me, I have people to see."

"There's a manipulative woman if ever I met one," remarked Edna as Iris walked away.

"I thought she was quite forthcoming. And I admire her loyalty to her friend," said Horace.

"You're always taken in by a pretty face," Edna said, laughing.

"I agree with Horace," said Frederick. "Apart from the things she said about Jonny's death, she seems a nice sort. Marjorie told us how she defended Jonny when this Sir Andrew objected to his presence. That's not someone who's manipulative, but someone who tries to keep the peace."

"Since when did you become an expert in female psychology?" Edna retorted.

In order to prevent a sparring match, Marjorie intervened. "At least we know now that Frederick was right to be suspicious. Jonny Sebastian was murdered. I'm not convinced he was together enough to come up with an elaborate suicide plan to incriminate Sir Andrew, and he wouldn't have arranged to meet Frederick if he intended to take his own life that morning. We need to know what evidence the police have against Sir Andrew."

"Not enough to arrest him straight away, or they would have done so. It's only because he riled them that they did that," Edna said.

"True. So, the question is," said Horace, "do we believe Andrew is innocent?"

"Well, I do," said Edna, glaring at Frederick. "And before you argue, I'm the one who looked into his eyes yesterday. I'm sure his superior attitude makes him enemies and he might give the impression he could get angry enough to kill, but if he were to kill someone, it would be a temper thing. Not one that involved drugging a man before trying to make his death look like an accident."

"Edna makes a good point," said Marjorie. "Iris Flame – like so many we have spoken to – is hiding something. I don't know what, but she was physically trembling when the police were here. Her reaction to their presence raises more questions than answers. I'd like to know what the fallout between Michael Sebastian and her husband was all about."

"Michael's ex-girlfriend, Sylvia Swann, would be on Jonny's hit list I'm sure," said Horace.

"Oh yes," said Marjorie. "We do need to speak to her again. Perhaps Frederick and I can have a word with her while you and Edna speak to the coach, Oswald Greene. If there were rumours flying around Henley at the time Michael died, I'm sure a man in his position would have heard."

"That's an excellent idea, but first I need caffeine," said Edna, starting towards the Coffee and Ices Garden.

"I wouldn't mind a coffee myself," said Horace.

"And a pot of tea wouldn't hurt," added Marjorie.

Frederick exhaled a frustrated sigh, but didn't argue.

EIGHTEEN

Horace and Edna hustled their way through the bustling crowds to get a glimpse of the finishing line. There were no vacant seats, so Horace laid his jacket on the grass so they could watch the end of the next race while keeping a lookout for Oswald Greene.

They were soon caught up in the rivalry between three universities racing neck and neck, each team dripping sweat as they tried to increase their stroke rate. Horace shielded his eyes with a hand to protect them from the sun's glare while cheering for the Bristol team.

"Why are you cheering for them?" Edna asked.

"I don't know. For Frederick... and Jonny. They both went to Bristol University." He was hoarse from shouting when Bristol took the win and was about to suggest they get a cold drink when Edna nudged him.

"Over there."

He followed her pointing finger and spotted the man they were looking for. Oswald was tall and wiry with bronzed skin, fit looking despite being in his early-to-mid seventies.

"Time for our chat then," Horace said.

He helped Edna up from the ground and carried his blazer over his shoulder while they strolled to the edge of a private section where crews and coaches mingled.

Edna hesitated. "We should wait here."

"Why?"

Edna's wide eyes were on the No Entry sign leading to the beehives. Horace placed his blazer around her shoulders.

"It'll be okay."

"It had better be. Promise we'll steer clear of those."

"Stay close to me." Horace deftly passed the beehives, keeping Edna between the hives and the hedge before he urged her to take a right turn down a hedge-lined path. He kept Oswald's burgundy jacket in sight.

Oswald took a left behind the boathouse.

"Hang on a minute, Horace. What's he up to?" Edna whispered.

Horace stopped dead and they remained concealed behind a hedge, watching to see where Oswald would go next. Reginald Blackwood soon appeared and the men started an intense discussion, trying hard to keep their voices low.

"What's that all about?" said Horace.

"Can you hear anything?"

"No. We need to get closer, but there's only one way."

Edna's eyes popped out on stalks. "Don't tell me: the hives."

"I'm afraid so. Come on." Horace retraced their steps along the hedged path and walked slowly behind the beehives, urging her to follow. "You'll be fine as long as they don't think we're a threat."

"Not reassuring, Horace. And what if Ossie and Reggie think we're a threat? We might be attacked twice."

Horace grinned. "You're safe with me, but we need to get a move on. Things are heating up by the sounds of it."

As they took another path to get within a few feet of the

men, tempers were flaring and they were no longer controlling the volume.

Horace and Edna crouched behind another hedge.

"I'm not letting Andrew take the blame for something you did. Either you tell them, or I will," Reginald spoke through gritted teeth, his face contorted.

Oswald's eyes narrowed, his jaw sharpening. "I don't know what you're talking about. What about you? You always had a thing for Sylvia. Who's to say you didn't kill Michael and then Jonny?"

"That's the most stupid thing you've ever said," Reginald spat back. "There's no point hiding. You're responsible, and you know it. You've got until noon."

Reginald turned to walk away, but Oswald's hand shot out, grabbing his arm, spinning him back around. The sudden movement caused Edna to gasp. Horace placed a finger to his lips.

"Shush."

With fists clenched, Reginald growled, "You'd better let go, old man."

Oswald's eyes flashed with fury. In an instant, he swung a punch, connecting with Reginald's face. The impact resulted in a loud thud.

Reginald stumbled, but regained his footing. His hand went to his lip, which was trickling with blood. For a moment, he stared in shock, then let out a roar and lunged at Oswald, wrestling him to the ground.

Oswald, despite his age, was strong, but Reginald had the advantage of weight. The two men crashed into a nearby shrubbery, leaves and twigs flying as they continued their struggle. Reginald pinned Oswald to the ground, raising his fist, ready to strike.

"Stop this at once!" Horace's authoritative voice boomed as he stepped from behind the hedge and pulled Reginald away from Oswald. "Fighting behind the boathouse, gentlemen? I suggest this ends now before I report you both to the authorities."

His intervention was enough to prevent tempers from flaring any further and bring calm to the situation.

"Sorry," Reginald said to Oswald, offering a hand to help the older man up. Both were breathing heavily, their smart clothes dishevelled and grass stained.

"Me too," Oswald replied, straightening his blazer.

Horace eyed them both. "Perhaps you could explain what this is all about over a drink," he said, his tone making it clear he wasn't asking.

The two men exchanged a look before nodding. "It's time," said Reginald.

Looking like two naughty schoolboys caught smoking behind the bike sheds, Oswald and Reginald walked with their heads down in front of Horace and Edna.

Edna leaned in and whispered in Horace's ear, "Well, that was more exciting than any of the boat races so far. I wouldn't want to cross you."

Horace chuckled. "Let's hope the explanation for the friction is just as thrilling. I've got a feeling we might be getting nearer to concluding our case."

Now that they didn't have to stay hidden, they took the long route, bypassing the beehives, and arrived at the Bridge Bar Garden. Horace bought the two men pints, but he and Edna settled for iced tea.

Once they were all seated, an uncomfortable silence descended. Horace took a sip of his drink, then set the glass down with a deliberate clonk.

"Okay," he said, shifting his gaze from one to the other. "What's the story?"

Reginald, holding a napkin to nurse his still-bleeding lip, spoke first. "I heard the police arrested Sir Andrew earlier. They suspect he killed Jonny."

"And yet you were the one arguing with him the night before he died," said Edna, eyes narrowing.

Reginald's shoulders slumped. "If he'd listened to me, he'd still be alive."

"What exactly did you say to him?" Horace leaned forward.

"I already told you. I suggested he leave Henley and forget about Michael's death. But he just wouldn't listen. He was convinced there was more to it, and that Michael had been murdered. And now the police believe Jonny was murdered."

"Was he right about Michael?" Edna asked, her voice uncharacteristically gentle.

Reginald's silence spoke volumes.

Oswald cleared his throat, his hand tightening around his beer glass. "Michael wasn't murdered. There's more to it than a simple accident, but not in the way Jonny thought." He took a deep breath. "It was my fault."

Horace and Edna exchanged glances. "What do you mean?" Horace asked.

Oswald's voice cracked as he said, "I killed him. It was my training methods... They led to his death."

Reginald nodded. "I suspected it for years but kept it to myself. Oswald's coaching methods drove Michael to drink. Michael was too sensitive, that's why he drowned."

Horace was having difficulty processing this assertion. "Coaching methods?"

"I was well-known for my unorthodox training techniques. I pushed the rowers hard, sometimes too hard. Michael had a lot of skill... He was a star pupil... but he was also precious."

"I remember those days," Reginald added. "Oswald's training regimes were brutal. Most of us could take it, but Michael... He got low on it, started taking every criticism to heart."

"I didn't realise the effect it was having on him," said Oswald.

Edna's brow furrowed. "Seriously? You were amateur rowers. You were hardly training for the Olympics, so what makes you think that's what drove him to drink? And even if it did, you weren't responsible for his death."

"You don't understand." Oswald took a long swig of his beer. "The night before he died, before the rest of the team arrived... when he showed up drunk, I... I said some terrible things to him. I told him he was a disgrace and threatened to throw him off the team if he didn't pull himself together. He was about to set up a work team and wanted me to train them, but I refused, saying if they were all drunken louts like him, he could forget it."

"As I told you, I more or less said the same thing when he showed up again later," said Reginald. "Told him he couldn't train with us. He stormed off, furious."

"And the next morning, he was found dead," said Horace.

"I've carried that guilt ever since. I carried on coaching for a few years and still do... in an advisory capacity... but I'm much more careful how I treat people."

Reginald placed a hand on Oswald's shoulder. "We all played a part in it. If I'd gone after him that night, he might have been okay."

"But neither of you killed him," Edna pointed out.

Reginald dabbed his lip again. "We might just as well have done. We set the accident in motion. And now, with Jonny's death, it's brought it all back again. When I heard Andrew had been arrested, I wanted Oswald to come clean."

"But I was afraid of the consequences."

"Pardon me for not following this guilt trip," said Edna. "But what the heck has this got to do with Jonny's death?"

Horace finished his iced tea. "I have to agree with Edna, I can't see what any of this has to do with Jonny's death or Andrew's arrest for it, unless you killed Jonny as well."

Oswald reeled back. "No! Of course not."

"Well then. You see, we believe Jonny was right that somebody killed Michael."

"And the same person killed Jonny all these years later," Edna said.

Oswald's brow furrowed; he wiped sweat from his forehead with a handkerchief. "Do you really believe that? Because if that's the case, Michael's death had nothing to do with me."

Reginald sighed heavily. "You're forgetting they both had drink problems, and I might have saved Jonny in the same way I could have saved Michael if I'd tried to help rather than driving him away."

Horace shook his head. "No. There's more to these deaths than alcohol. We know Jonny was a strong swimmer and was familiar with the currents. What's more, Jonny asked Fred to meet him on the morning he died to tell him something."

"And you think that whatever he was going to tell your friend got him killed?" Oswald seemed brighter. It was odd to be happy about a suspicious death, but as he'd been carrying the burden of a man's drowning on his shoulders for two decades, it made sense.

"Whatever you believe or don't believe, Sir Andrew isn't a killer," said Reginald. "He's annoying at times and doesn't suffer fools, but he's not someone who goes around murdering people. Besides, he has less motive than any of us."

"What about your crush on Sylvia Swann?" Edna asked.

Reginald's head shot towards her.

"Sorry. We heard the row between you two," said Horace.

"It's nothing to do with any of this. I liked her back in the day, but she chose Michael. It was annoying, him being married at the time, but I wouldn't have killed anybody over it. Besides, I moved on."

Oswald's face told a different story, but perhaps the follow up was better left to a later date, thought Horace.

"Can you think of anyone else who wouldn't want their past unearthed by Jonny's digging?"

"No. And I find it hard to believe that anyone killed Michael," said Oswald. "Or Jonny for that matter."

"Well, I hate to spell it out for you," snapped Edna, "but as you know, Sir Andrew was arrested this morning. We witnessed it, and the police mentioned Jonny was drugged before being held under the water, so I suggest you start thinking hard, because if Sir Andy Flirty-Gertie is innocent, they might be coming for one of you two next."

Reginald's eyes widened. "I didn't know that."

"You mentioned a hit-and-run accident," said Horace. "Did Jonny say anything about that to either of you?"

Oswald rubbed his neck. "Now you come to mention it, he asked me about it. He knew a lot of people open up to me and asked if anyone had ever confided in me."

"And did they?" Edna pressed.

"No. If they had done, I would have reported it to the police, but he seemed to think the driver was local and that there had been a cover up. I didn't take much notice, to be honest."

"Did he mention a name?" Horace asked.

"Not that I recall, half of what Jonny said didn't make sense."

Reginald was shifting in his seat. "Look, thanks for the drink and all that, but we need to go. Come on, Oswald."

Once the two men had left, Edna snapped, "What a pair of idiots."

"Not necessarily," said Horace. "If neither of them believed what Jonny was saying about Michael's death, they might well have surmised that Oswald had pushed him too hard."

"Why did they take their rowing so seriously? It was just a hobby."

Horace knew that explaining the rowing subculture to Edna would lead to further derision, so he didn't try.

"Interesting that Jonny was mentioning the hit-and-run, though, eh?"

"Yes," said Horace. "It appears Marjorie's right and that's the lead to follow."

"Could Andrew have been driving that night?"

"It's worth looking into. Come on, Edna. It's time for lunch. Let's meet the others and see what they've found out."

NINETEEN

Frederick was moving slower than usual, a pensive look on his face.

"Is everything all right?" Marjorie asked.

"Not really."

"Don't worry. We'll find out who killed your friend."

"I suppose it's that bit I'm finding hard to digest. It's fine believing something might have happened, but knowing... Well, that's a different thing entirely."

"It must be hard," said Marjorie, looping her arm through his, "but now justice needs to be served."

Frederick stopped to look at her, his grey eyes misting over. "You're right. But I'm finding the whole matter a confusing jumble of events that may or may not have anything to do with each other. Do you really suppose that the three deaths are linked?"

They had to be. Other than a boating rivalry escalating out of hand, it was the only thing making any sense. "If somebody at the heart of the community was responsible for Casper Wolff's death, then what began as a matter of not reporting an accident might have spiralled out of control. Indeed, the driver – if we're right – has demonstrated that they are willing to kill to keep their secret safe."

"So it's become a matter of life and death to them? Why didn't they just own up?"

Marjorie considered the question carefully. "I really can't answer that. Most people wouldn't have driven on in the first place. Alcohol could have been involved and they feared being arrested, or they were frightened of losing a reputation."

"Even if that were the case, sentences weren't that severe for causing death by dangerous driving twenty years ago."

"There's still a lot of work to be done in that area, but that's an argument for another day. I can only imagine that this terrible secret has hung over this person's life for decades. And, as you say, it has led them down a dark path. They are desperate enough to kill not once but twice, to keep what they did secret."

Shouts filled the air around them as another race drew to a conclusion.

"Before tracking down Sylvia, shall we see if Dr Christie has any more information than what we overheard?" Frederick said.

"That would be a good start. Please, lead the way."

"We'll find her in the smoking enclosure."

"One forgets doctors can have the same vices as us mere mortals," said Marjorie, chuckling. "I'm looking forward to meeting the prickly doctor."

Frederick smiled, his eyes brightening in the sun. "Then follow me."

They hadn't quite reached the designated smoking area when Frederick drew to a halt. "There she is by the first aid tent."

Marjorie observed a woman of average height in her late sixties, who had a slight stoop. Despite that, she was strong enough to lift a crate from the top of a pile, checking the contents of the one beneath it. She pointed to something and a woman in a St John Ambulance uniform nodded and lifted out a box.

A younger man in his forties took the box from the St John Ambulance worker and inspected the contents. The first aider was called away to attend to someone while Dr Christie and the man exchanged a few words. The man turned and stomped away from the doctor.

Dr Christie returned the box to its crate.

"I see what you mean. Judging by that man's reaction, Dr Christie has a way with words."

"Hello again."

Dr Christie jumped when Frederick spoke. She turned around, glaring at him. "You shouldn't sneak up on people like that."

Frederick's neck reddened. "Sorry. I didn't mean to startle you."

"Well, you did! What do you want?"

"Erm. We met yesterday. You said you might be able to have a word with the pathologist."

"And I also said I might not, and that if I discovered anything I would contact you. Is this how you return a favour?"

Marjorie felt the need to step in. "If this is a bad time, we could come back later."

As if seeing Marjorie for the first time, Dr Christie appraised her. "Who are you?"

"This is a friend of mine, Lady Marjorie Snellthorpe," said Frederick. "I really am sorry if I've upset you."

Dr Christie sighed heavily, gazing in the direction of the man she'd been talking to as he entered the tent. "You haven't. Not really. I'm less tolerant of interruptions these days."

"You look in need of a cup of tea," said Marjorie. "Would it be okay to have a word?"

"I'm busy and I don't have anything to report."

"Ah, but we do," said Marjorie. "It won't take long."

Dr Christie hesitated before nodding. "All right. I could do with a strong coffee."

Once seated in the gardens away from the designated smoking area, Dr Christie looked at Frederick. "I've been busy and really haven't managed to speak to anyone from the hospital yet."

Marjorie doubted the good doctor had any intention of trying to do so and suspected she had fobbed Frederick off in order to get rid of him.

"We've discovered Frederick's friend, Jonny Sebastian, had been sedated and held under the water. The police are now treating the death as suspicious. They were here first thing this morning."

Dr Christie almost spilled her coffee and had to replace the cup to its saucer. "You mean he was murdered?"

"It appears that way," said Frederick.

"You don't hear about such things happening in Henley," said Dr Christie. "Who would have thought?"

"Someone mentioned Jonny had upset a number of people before he died," said Marjorie. "We believe one of those people may have killed him."

"I find that difficult to believe. If we all went around killing those who upset us, there wouldn't be many people alive."

In her case, Marjorie could believe it. "Nevertheless, that appears to be the case."

"Why on earth would anyone do that?"

"It all stems from his cousin, Michael," said Frederick. "You told me you knew Michael, and that Jonny asked you about him?"

Dr Christie's lips tightened. "And I told him I believed the coroner's conclusion was correct. I don't see how the two deaths are connected."

"Someone said Jonny had upset you."

"Henley is full of gossipmongers. I suggest you take with a pinch of salt what most people say around here."

"Did he?"

Dr Christie stared at Marjorie as she lifted her coffee cup to her lips. Light brown nicotine-stained fingers gripped the handle as she took a sip and placed it back down. "It takes a lot to upset me, but if you mean did he annoy me, yes, he did, though no more than most people. I no longer feel the need to put up with people I don't like and although I didn't know Jonny Sebastian well, I didn't particularly like him. He drank too much."

"You said you hardly knew him at all when we spoke," said Frederick.

"That still stands. I didn't mention not liking him because I realised you had just lost an old friend."

"You weren't going to speak to the pathologist, were you?" Frederick sounded gloomy.

"I didn't think it was worth it, if I'm being honest. I've asked around, though, and most people are of the same opinion as I am, that he fell into the water inebriated. If what you say is correct, they... and I... may have assumed wrong. I hope you find what you're looking for, Mr Mackworth, but just because sedatives were found doesn't point to murder. Trust me, a lot of people take medication, both legitimately and illegally. It may still turn out to be a senseless accident, or even suicide. He wouldn't be the first to take a handful of pills and wash them down with alcohol."

"The police have arrested Sir Andrew Eccles," said Frederick, sounding belligerent.

"This gets worse. Why on earth would they do that?"

"Perhaps because he found Michael Sebastian's body and was in the vicinity where Jonny was found," said Marjorie.

A concerned frown appeared on Dr Christie's face. "I've just remembered something."

"What?"

"The pathologist mentioned after Michael's death they found diazepam in his system. Not enough to kill him, but it was assumed that the mixture of that and alcohol led to his death. It was kept out of the news for the family's sake."

"Surely it was mentioned at the inquest?" Marjorie said.

"Of course, but few people attended and it wasn't mentioned in the newspapers. The reporter was a friend of the family. As I said, nobody thought much of it at the time. Diazepam was commonly prescribed before better drugs came along. Michael was registered with one of my more 'old-school' colleagues, based in Reading." Dr Christie gazed into the distance. "I can't believe Andrew could have any involvement in Jonny's death."

"What about the hit-and-run accident?" Frederick asked.

Colour drained from Dr Christie's face before she answered in a tremulous voice. "I don't know how you heard about that, but it has no bearing on any of this. Iris Flame told me Jonny Sebastian had unearthed an old news story and convinced himself that Michael had been killed because of it. In my opinion, Jonny was unhinged following the loss of his wife. What he needed was grief counselling – I suggested as much to him – but I'm told he was determined to follow conspiracy theories instead.

"Ask anyone who lived in Henley at the time of the motoring accident. Michael was too ambitious to let his employee's death bother him. In all the time I knew him, he only mentioned it once and that was after the funeral. The police concluded the accident was caused by a youth, or group of youths. I don't know if they ever found who was involved. If Jonny and/or Michael were killed, I would look much closer to home if I were you."

"But—"

"Dr Christie has a point, Frederick. We know they both were good at falling out with people."

"I'm pleased someone has sense around here. Now, if you'll excuse me, I have some races to watch."

With Dr Christie in the distance, Frederick asked, "You don't really believe the hit-and-run is now out of the equation, do you?"

"It's hard to say, but if the good doctor says Michael wasn't concerned by his friend's death, perhaps Jonny was looking down the wrong rabbit hole. I suggest you call that reporter to see what she says about it. I'll see if I can track down Sylvia Swann. If anyone knows what was going on in Michael's head, it has to be his lover."

Marjorie's own head felt as if it might explode as Frederick left her finishing her tea.

TWENTY

Frederick's head had just hit the pillow when his phone buzzed. Reaching out, he swiped the screen, the harsh light momentarily blinding him in the darkened room. He blinked, focussing on the message that appeared:

> I hear you're looking into a historic hit-and-run. I have information but will be leaving Henley soon. Meet me in twenty minutes where Jonathan Sebastian's body was found. You know the place.

His heart raced as he reread the anonymous text. It must be from the reporter he'd been trying all day to contact. This could be the breakthrough they needed.

Other than what Horace had revealed about Oswald's guilt trip, and Frederick and Marjorie's conversation with Dr Christie, the rest of the day had been unproductive. Marjorie hadn't managed to find Sylvia Swann, and the four friends had ended up watching the afternoon's races, which had been a pleasant interlude from the investigation that was puzzling them all.

With every step forward, there were more going backwards. Perhaps now Frederick had a chance to find out what had happened to Casper Wolff, and Michael Sebastian.

Sleep forgotten, Frederick swung his legs out of bed, fully alert. He hurriedly dressed in the clothes he'd hung on the back of the chair in his room: dark trousers and a short-sleeved shirt. As a last-minute addition, with the temperature in his room dropping, he pulled on a navy jumper before donning his jacket.

As he buttoned his jacket and stared at his shoes, doubts crept in. Should he wake the others? There wasn't time – whoever sent the message was in a hurry. And if he was honest with himself, a small part of him relished the idea of cracking the case on his own.

Compromising, Frederick scribbled a hasty note on the hotel notepad:

Gone to meet informant about hit-and-run at the bridge where Jonny found. It's just gone midnight. Back soon. – F

He tiptoed along the corridor, wincing at every creak of the floorboards until he arrived outside of Marjorie's room. He pushed the note under the door before creeping downstairs. When he got to the front door, he released the breath he'd been subconsciously holding, and placed his shoes on the ground, slipping his feet into them and bending down to lace them up. He took his coat off the hook in the hall and looked back. The hotel was silent. All the guests were long retired for the night.

Leaving the hotel, he started down the drive into the pitch-black night, interspersed with lights and bangs from fireworks. He felt the chill of the air. The weather was changing and the clouds felt dark and foreboding. Frederick pulled his jacket collar up to cover his neck and fastened his coat.

At the end of the drive, he hesitated. The road beyond looked uninviting. For a moment, his resolve wavered. *This is madness*, a sensible voice in his head warned. *You're not cut out for cloak-and-dagger meetings in the dead of night.*

But then he thought of Jonny – hurting, complicated Jonny – whose life had been snuffed out just as he was on the verge of uncovering the truth about his cousin. Frederick owed it to his old friend to see this through. Taking a deep breath, he stepped forward.

The streets of Henley were deserted, a far cry from the bustling crowds of the daytime, and the fireworks were becoming more distant. Frederick's footsteps echoed on the pavement as he retraced the route he and Marjorie had taken that fateful morning. Back then, the horror of Jonny's body being pulled from the river had overshadowed everything else. Now, he had time to take in his surroundings.

The quaint shops and cafés that lined the main street were shuttered and dark. Occasionally, a splash of light spilled from an upstairs window, hinting at late-night revellers or insomniacs. A black cat, startled by Frederick's approach, darted across his path, making his heart leap in his chest. The cat disappeared into a shadowy alley.

Frederick's hand reached out for a nearby lamppost to steady himself. The tower of St Mary's Church loomed ahead, its outline just visible against the overcast sky. Frederick's gaze was drawn upwards, tracing the path where stone met clouds. For a moment, he felt a profound sense of his own insignificance in the face of centuries of history. Trying not to think of the spooky stories Sylvia and the man in the graveyard had told him and Horace, he took deep breaths. In. Out. In. Out. He repeated the words inside his head with every step forward.

As he neared the river, a damp mist curled around his ankles, or was it his imagination? The air grew heavy with the scent of algae and mud. Frederick pulled his coat tighter. He'd left in such a rush he'd forgotten to bring a hat.

He felt a shiver running down his spine.

A sudden gust of wind set the trees rustling, and Frederick's nerve almost failed him. This was madness. He should turn back, wake the others, reply to the text and approach this sensibly in the light of day. But even as the thought formed, his feet carried him onwards. He was so close now.

"*Be brave, Frederick.*" He recalled his mother's words on his first day of school. It was as if she knew he would be tormented and bullied because of his small frame and studious nature. He'd survived school and he would survive this.

The bridge materialised out of the gloom, its graceful arches spanning the inky water below. Frederick paused at the foot of the bridge, straining his eyes for any sign of his mysterious informant. Nothing moved in the night's stillness.

Another sense of foreboding tried to stop him in his tracks, but he wasn't going to allow it to do so. For once in his life, Frederick Mackworth was going to be the hero. Soon he would know what had happened all those years ago. No more teasing from Edna. And his friends could get on and enjoy the last two days of the regatta without distraction.

Gathering his courage, Frederick began crossing the bridge. His footsteps sounded unnaturally loud on the stonework, and he found himself trying to walk more quietly, though he couldn't have said why.

Halfway across, he stopped. Something felt off. The hairs on the back of his neck stood up, and despite the mist hovering over the bridge from the water below, he had the distinct impression of being watched. Frederick turned slowly, peering into the shadows on both sides of the bridge.

Nothing.

Quashing his fear, he put one foot in front of the other. Apart from the sound of his heartbeat threatening to burst through his chest, all he could hear were his own footsteps and the gentle lapping of the river below. With his feet feeling like lead weights, he continued to the other side. Stepping onto the ground where he'd last seen the body of his friend, Frederick felt emboldened by his mission.

"Hello?" he called softly, his voice sounding thin and reedy in the black night. "It's Frederick Mackworth. I'm here about the hit-and-run incident."

Silence mocked him. Then, from somewhere to his right, came the faintest rustle of movement.

"Hello?" Frederick said again, edging towards the sound. "It's okay, I'm alone. You can trust me."

He leaned forward, trying to see if someone was concealed in the tangle of willow branches below. The mist had thickened, obscuring his view of the riverbank. Frederick squinted, willing his eyes to penetrate the fog.

There – was that a flash of movement? He took another step forward, balancing precariously on the edge of the river as he craned his neck for a better look.

The push in his back was so sudden and unexpected that Frederick had no time to cry out. One moment he was peering into the gloom, the next he was falling, tumbling down the bank with an unstoppable velocity and a sickening lurch in his stomach.

He hit the water with a tremendous splash, the icy shock seizing the air in his lungs. Panicking, Frederick flailed wildly, his sodden clothes dragging him under. The current was stronger than he'd imagined, already sweeping him away from the edge. He wished now he was as good a swimmer as Jonny had been.

As he struggled to keep his head above water, Frederick caught a glimpse of a dark figure retreating from the bridge's edge. Then a wave slapped him in the face, and he went under, choking and spluttering in the murky depths of the Thames.

TWENTY-ONE

Marjorie was woken by the sound of fireworks. Switching on the bedside lamp, she sat up in bed feeling aches and pains that hadn't been there the day before. The deckchairs at the regatta, though comfortable when she was sitting, were a challenge to get in and out of.

She picked up her watch and scrunched her eyes to see the time: 2am. Horace had mentioned a VIP party involving a number of celebrities which formed part of the regatta. As the lights from the fireworks flashed in the distance, she wondered if it was coming to an end.

Now she was awake, sleep was going to be difficult to come by, so she swung her legs over the side of the bed and strolled to the window. She could see fireworks where the starting line was. They were loud and intrusive.

It must drive the locals who have to go to work the next day mad.

Marjorie straightened her back and moved her arms above her head before stretching from side to side. Keeping herself fit enough to enjoy what time was left to her was one of her main goals in life. She had attended far too many funerals over the past twelve months, which had caused her to consider her mortality. In her head, she was still in her forties, but her body had a nasty habit of reminding her that the years were passing by.

"Really, Snellthorpe. Stop this line of thought. You're fitter than many people twenty years younger. Go back to bed." She needed to heed her own advice. There was a nip in the air tonight and as she looked towards the river, a mist obscured the view, leaving only shadows. The fireworks wouldn't help that. Marjorie reluctantly closed the window, shutting out the night breeze.

Flashing blue emergency lights were visible in the distance. Marjorie strained to see where they were going. They were heading to Henley Bridge. Her breath caught in her throat as thoughts of Frederick's friend drifted into her head. Drowning in ice-cold water must have been terrifying. She hoped the sedatives had removed all consciousness from his brain. She had read about drowning and knew that most people's hearts gave out from the cold before they inhaled water, which was a blessing in disguise.

Shaking such thoughts from her head, Marjorie turned back towards the bed. That's when she saw the note under her door.

She picked it up and, after switching the light on, she donned her reading glasses. Her hand flew to her chest and she gasped as she read the words.

With her heart racing, Marjorie reached for her phone only to realise the battery had died. "Blast!" She scrambled around looking for the charger and found it in her suitcase.

"When will you learn to keep your phone on charge?" Her son Jeremy's voice rang in her head. *"One day you're going to miss an emergency."* Marjorie hadn't dared tell him that she'd already missed several for that very reason. And still she hadn't learned her lesson! As she plugged the wretched thing in and switched it on, she vowed to do better.

Once the signal was there, she dialled Frederick's number. Straight to voicemail.

"Breathe, Marjorie. He's probably asleep."

She pulled on her dressing gown and left her room. Moving stealthily towards Frederick's, she tapped on the door, telephoning again at the same time while putting her ear to the keyhole.

Nothing.

Frederick was like her and often switched his phone off at night, so it might not mean anything.

Now what?

At that moment, Horace opened his door and peered out. "Marjorie! Are you all right?"

"I was trying to get Frederick."

Horace's brow furrowed as he looked at his watch. "Why? Is there something the matter?"

"He left a note under my door."

Horace rubbed sleep from his eyes. "And?"

"It appears he left for a clandestine meeting shortly after midnight. I wanted to check he was back. Wait there."

By the time Marjorie had collected the note and returned, Horace had donned his dressing gown. He beckoned her into his room just as another door opened.

"What's going on?" Edna hissed.

"Not here," said Horace. "Come inside."

It worried Marjorie that both Horace and Edna had awoken, but not Frederick. She consoled herself with the fact he'd told her he was a deep sleeper. Then she remembered the flashing blue lights. Were the two things connected?

Edna somehow managed to look as though she had been awake and ready to go out for the day, apart from her wig being slightly skewed. When they were all in his room and the door was closed, Horace read the note and passed it to Edna.

"What was he thinking?" Horace said.

"He doesn't think. That's his problem," said Edna.

"I know where Dinah keeps the master key. I'll fetch it and check Fred's room. Back in a jiffy." Horace disappeared leaving Marjorie worried sick, not helped by Edna's mutterings that if anything had happened to Frederick, it would be his own silly fault.

Marjorie was relieved when Horace returned, but the look on his face spoke volumes. "He's not in his room. Try phoning again."

Marjorie did as instructed, but once more, the phone went straight to voicemail. "I saw blue lights by the bridge a while ago. What if it was a trap?"

"Phone the police, Marge." Despite her initial reaction, Edna's eyes betrayed her own fear that something bad had happened to Frederick.

Marjorie managed to get through to the police to ask if there had been any accidents near Henley Bridge.

"Who's asking?" a tired-sounding desk sergeant quizzed.

"My name is Lady Marjorie Snellthorpe. I don't have time to go into details, but I believe a friend of mine is in mortal danger. His name is Frederick Mackworth."

"Just a minute." Irritating music rang out.

"Put it on speaker, Marge," said Edna.

"Erm..."

"Here. Let me do it." Edna grabbed the phone and pressed a button. The music filled the room for a few minutes before a female voice came on the line.

"Is that Lady Marjorie?"

"Yes."

"This is PC Fry. Your friend has been taken to the Oxford Radcliffe Infirmary. We've been trying to contact his next-of-kin. Do you have their details?"

Marjorie found herself unable to speak, her breath was being sucked out of her.

"This is Horace Tyler. I'm with Lady Marjorie. How bad is it?"

"He hasn't regained consciousness. Get to the hospital and someone will meet you there. My sergeant is—"

Horace ended the call.

"We'll take my car," he said, heading for the door.

"Don't you think we should put some clothes on?" Edna gave a nervous chuckle.

"Of course. Let's meet downstairs in five minutes."

It was actually twenty minutes before they were all dressed and assembled, ready to go. Marjorie's emotions were all over the place. One minute sheer terror gripped her heart and the next anger at Frederick for being so foolhardy. And as for the person who'd lured him into a trap, they would pay.

TWENTY-TWO

A deathly pale face was all that was visible beneath the silver blanket the ward sister explained was designed to bring Frederick's body temperature back up to normal. Through the viewing window, Marjorie saw a nurse tending machines and drips.

"He's lucky to be alive," the sister explained.

"Just one visitor," the police officer outside the side room said.

Marjorie entered. The nurse introduced herself as Marion and continued her work while Marjorie sat upright in the visitor's chair. There she watched on, a helpless spectator of a process completely out of her control. It wasn't a feeling she was familiar with and Marjorie didn't like it one bit.

She was relieved when Horace popped his head around the door. "I'll take over here for a bit. The detectives would like a word with you."

"He'll be okay," said Marion. "His core temperature's rising. I suspect he's stronger than he looks."

With that, and the nurse's reassuring smile in mind, Marjorie stood up and headed to the door. Horace squeezed her arm.

"He's a fighter, Marjorie."

When she got into the waiting room, Edna thrust a polystyrene cup into her hand. "Here, Marge, drink this."

"Thank you." Edna's sympathy was almost too much to bear. "The nurse says he's going to recover."

"Of course he is," Edna said, although her tone wasn't as convincing as her words. "There's a couple of detectives waiting through there." She pointed to the sister's office.

The sergeant who had arrested Sir Andrew sat with DC Briar.

"Sorry to disturb you at such a time, but we want to find out who did this to your friend. This is Detective Sergeant Cramer, she's been looking into Jonny Sebastian's death," said Briar.

"Frederick was pushed into the river then?"

"Yes. It's lucky a fisherman heard the splash and disturbed the person, or it could have been much worse," said Sergeant Cramer, appraising Marjorie. "You were at the regatta when we took Sir Andrew Eccles in for questioning." It was a statement rather than a question.

"We all were. My friends and I raised suspicions about Mr Sebastian's death but no-one took us seriously." Marjorie held the sergeant's gaze.

Cramer cleared her throat. "Your friends say Mr Mackworth received a text from someone claiming to know something about a hit-and-run accident twenty-two years ago. Do you know who sent the message?"

"If I did, you would be the first to know."

Cramer sighed. Marjorie was angry and wasn't going to let the police off lightly. "Let me put it another way, Lady Snellthorpe. Who had Mr Mackworth's mobile phone number?"

Marjorie recalled Frederick handing out contact cards with his phone number on to all and sundry. "I'm afraid he gave it to a number of people. We were trying to find out what happened to his friend." Marjorie's chin jutted forward.

"I realise we could have acted sooner, but it would be most helpful if you cooperate with us now. Do you have names of the people he gave his number? It might help us to gather a list and check alibis."

Marjorie's mind whizzed back over the past few days. "I can tell you the people we spoke to and we can assume each had his number. There was Reginald Blackwood and Oswald Greene, but we've already eliminated them as suspects—"

The audible sigh suggested the sergeant didn't have time for her continuing to play amateur detective, but at least she had the courtesy not to say as much.

"Then there was Sir Andrew Eccles, but you have him in custody."

"No. His solicitor was on the case as soon as we got to the station. We didn't have enough evidence to hold him," said Briar, his voice tinged with regret.

"Anyone else?" Cramer asked.

"Iris Flame, a local benefactor and wealthy widow, and Sylvia Swann, Michael Sebastian's ex-lover. He also gave it to Dr Elsa Christie."

"Is that everyone?"

"He'd spent most of yesterday trying to contact a former reporter, Sharon Taylor. She covered the hit-and-run accident my friends mentioned, but she's retired to Brighton."

"I might regret this," said Sergeant Cramer, "but what do you think the hit-and-run accident has to do with the death of his friend?"

"I'm sure Horace and Edna have already told you that our working theory is that Jonny's cousin Michael discovered who was driving the car that killed his friend and employee Casper Wolff. We believe that he may have confronted that person rather than going to the police and was killed as a result. At the time Michael died of his so-called accident, Jonny had been happily married and busy with his own life. For whatever reason, after his wife died, he decided to investigate his cousin's death. No doubt you will have found the newspaper articles in Jonny's house covering both Michael's death and the hit-and-run accident. My question to you is, why haven't you followed Jonny's research up?"

"I'd ask how you know what was in Mr Sebastian's house but we haven't got time for games. Mr Tyler told us about your visit to the family home."

"Touché, Sergeant. We don't know whether Jonny had uncovered evidence suggesting Michael was murdered, or whether it was a gut instinct, but he told Frederick he had something important to do in Henley before selling the family home. We believe it began with Michael and he found something that linked the hit-and-run to his death."

"What we know is that Mr Sebastian was throwing accusations at every person who knew his cousin. So, all he had was suspicions without evidence."

"I see. That ties in with what we've been hearing. In which case, Jonny Sebastian was fishing, hoping someone would take the bait."

"And if Michael was deliberately killed, the murderer took that bait, assuming he knew more than he did." The sergeant narrowed her eyes, staring at Marjorie. "What we don't know is what made you think Jonny Sebastian's death was foul play."

"Now I believe you're fishing, Sergeant. I told DC Briar and his colleague PC Fry, Frederick got a text in the middle of the night requesting he meet Jonny. Unfortunately, he was dead by the time we got there."

"It seems your friend gets a lot of texts in the middle of the night."

Marjorie glared at the sergeant. "We visited Jonny's home

because he told Frederick where he kept a spare key. It's as if he knew he might be in danger."

"We'll have to take your word on that. But you and your friends still entered what might have been a crime scene and you could have jeopardised our inquiry."

"Semantics, Sergeant. The fact of the matter is, we have managed to narrow the suspect list down."

"Let us be the judge of that. Mr Tyler has told us about his and Mrs Parkinton's conversation with Reginald Blackwood and Oswald Greene. And while it may seem unlikely they were involved, one man in particular was seen arguing with both Michael Sebastian and Jonny Sebastian on the nights before they died."

"Reginald. Yes, that's true, but what about the night of the hit-and-run?"

The sergeant eyed Marjorie once more. "After rowing practice, Mr Blackwood drove to Oxford and stayed in a hotel. He had early morning meetings the next day. We are checking his alibi, but you understand that records from that long ago are scant."

"I assume Sir Andrew also has an alibi, or you wouldn't have released him."

"First, let me say we are keeping an open mind about the hit-and-run being linked to the deaths."

Marjorie opened her mouth to protest but the sergeant raised a palm.

"It's one line of enquiry, but for all we know, Michael Sebastian died from a drunken fall. The only suspicious death we have to date is that of Jonny Sebastian and witnesses have told us he was miserable and took sedatives as well as drinking heavily."

"Did you know diazepam was found in Michael Sebastian's blood?"

Cramer's gaze shot to DC Briar, who shrugged helplessly. "Dare I ask how you know this?"

"Dr Christie mentioned it. Apparently, it was kept out of the press."

"That may be. DC Briar will re-check that autopsy report. We were leaning towards the suicide of an unhappy man with an axe to grind."

"Until tonight?"

"Yes. The text Mr Mackworth received means we will focus our attention on the hit-and-run. We haven't found his phone and assume it is in the Thames. If it's recovered and by some miracle we get it working again, I doubt the killer would have left their phone number for us. Life is never that easy."

"So we're back to alibis and who was driving the car on the night of the hit-and-run?"

"That's where we're stumped," said Briar. "All the people you mentioned, and others, have alibis for that night. There was an extensive investigation at the time. Michael Sebastian insisted upon it. There were two witnesses who had taken a shortcut through a field and swore they saw a dark Mercedes speeding along the Reading Road minutes after the accident. The car was weaving all over the road at more than eighty miles an hour. The police interviewed everyone in Henley who owned a dark Mercedes."

Marjorie felt her heart quicken. "And who on our list drove such a vehicle?"

"Oswald Greene, Iris Flame's husband Stefan, Sylvia Swann, Dr Christie and Michael Sebastian himself. Mercs were very popular in Henley at the time."

"Sir Andrew also owned one," said Briar, "although he wasn't questioned at the time because he was at home in Norfolk."

"And they all have alibis for the time of both Casper's and Michael's deaths, I suppose?"

Cramer didn't look at her. Instead, glaring at DC Briar, she said, "That's something we're checking. We will also be re-interviewing them all about the hit-and-run – apart from the deceased Stefan Flame, of course – but the initial investigation was thorough. On a dark night like that, it's also hard to say for certain that the witnesses were right about the colour or even the make of the car. Every garage in and around the area was checked for cars that had gone in for repairs and all the vehicles were examined."

"So, we have nothing." Marjorie was losing hope.

"We have one suspicious death and one attempted murder for fact. Which means we'll go through everything with a fine-tooth comb," said the sergeant.

"Did the fisherman who rescued Frederick see anything?"

"He saw a shadow in a dark coat but his attention was focussed on getting Mr Mackworth out of the water and calling an ambulance. We're hoping Mr Mackworth can tell us more when he wakes up. In the meantime, I've asked for an officer to be posted outside of his room."

"I saw. So, you think this person might try again?"

"If Mr Mackworth saw his attacker, most definitely, but if he didn't…" The sergeant shrugged. "But we're not taking any chances."

Anger she'd never experienced before surged through Marjorie's body when she got back to Frederick's room.

Horace was just coming out. "The doctor's been and says he should make a full recovery. They've sedated him for now and the police will make sure no-one else gets in the room. His oldest son's on the way. There's nothing more we can do here."

"Right," said Marjorie. "We have work to do."

Edna lifted her head when they entered the waiting room. "Uh oh. I recognise that look in your eyes, Marge. What do you have in mind?"

"We'll talk about it on the way back to Henley."

TWENTY-THREE

A tired trio met for breakfast, each feeling the aftereffects of their nightshift. After a light meal, because none of them felt much like eating, Horace waited for Marjorie to get the latest news from the hospital, and then he planned on calling Sharon Taylor, the reporter Frederick had tried to contact the day before.

Marjorie came back into the room as Horace and Edna were finishing coffees. He poured Marjorie a cup of strong tea.

"The ward staff wouldn't give me much information other than he was comfortable – you know how they can be when you're not a relative. Anyway, I insisted they let me speak to Frederick's son who arrived from Glasgow this morning. He says that his father is improving and that his core temperature has stabilised. Frederick's still drowsy from the medication – and most likely the shock – but there's some good news. The doctors believe he'll be moved to a less high-dependency bed later today."

"At least that's positive," said Edna. "I still can't believe he went traipsing off in the middle of the night, without telling anybody, to visit some random stranger who hadn't even left a name."

"We don't know the details of the message yet," said Marjorie, defensively. "Frederick must have had good reason to assume he would be safe."

Edna harrumphed, but Horace shot her a warning look not to say any more. They had all been worried and surprised about Frederick taking such a risk, but it was always easier to judge with the benefit of hindsight.

Marjorie seemed frail but determined, and Horace felt somehow responsible for what had happened. He finished his coffee before getting up.

"If you'll excuse me, I'll see if I can get hold of that reporter." He went into the small sitting room while most of the hotel guests were still enjoying Dinah's excellent breakfast.

Horace was proud of his granddaughter who had escaped a difficult marriage and set herself up in business. Horace and his oldest son had witnessed the effect her controlling husband had had on her, and they both had felt helpless to intervene, not knowing how bad things were. The catalyst had come when Dinah's ex had threatened their children. It spurred Dinah to ask for help and the family intervened, enabling her to take out a court order to keep him away from her and the children. The man hadn't gone down without a fight, blatantly lying in court, but testimony from Dinah's teenage children had been enough for her to win the case and file for divorce.

As far as Horace was aware, the ex still lived in Cardiff where he had taken up with someone else. Horace had given Dinah a loan to put down on the hotel and helped her set up the business in the early days. His granddaughter was a natural once she got her confidence back, and soon repaid what she owed. She now ran a successful business, his great grandchildren were settled in their new school and all had worked out for the best.

Horace's call went to the reporter's answering machine. He left a message just before Dinah came into the room with a cordless handset.

"There's a woman called Sharon Taylor on the phone asking to speak to Frederick."

"Thank you, Dinah. I'll take it." Horace grasped the phone. "Hello, this is Horace Tyler. I'm afraid Fred is in hospital, but if you're happy to talk, it's a matter of urgency. Fred wanted to ask you about your coverage of a hit-and-run accident twenty-two years ago."

"Yes, I got his messages. I was out all day yesterday. What do you want to know?"

"Any details about the accident that you remember, and whether you had any suspicions as to who was driving the car that killed Casper Wolff."

Sharon's response was cautious. "It was a long time ago, why are you so interested?"

Horace explained about Jonny Sebastian's death and how he had been investigating the death of his cousin, Michael Sebastian, who may in turn have been investigating the death of his friend, Casper. He also explained about Frederick being lured out in the early hours and pushed into the Thames.

"Thank God your friend is okay. I'm not sure how much help I can be. You seem to have a lot of ifs, buts and maybes, and I covered many stories during my time in Henley. The hit-and-run does stand out in my memory, though, because a lot of influential people pulled rank over it. It wouldn't surprise me if some of them knew who was driving the car that night. In my opinion, the police were sidetracked and didn't investigate it thoroughly. They were quick to point the finger elsewhere."

"Did anyone come under suspicion?" Horace asked.

"Yeah. There was a guy the police arrested. A car dealer. They believed he was guilty, but claimed he'd sold the car on or burned it out. That was their story and there wasn't enough evidence to make it stick."

"But you don't believe they were right?"

The line went silent for a moment before Sharon spoke again. "I haven't thought about it for years, but no, I didn't. My editor closed the story down when I started digging and put me on something else. Come to think of it, someone could have got to him."

"Who do you think they were covering for?"

"A few names kept cropping up at the time. Stefan Flame – he was an influential businessman with fingers in many pies, most of them corrupt if you ask me. Oswald Greene was reputed to drive like a maniac and sometimes under the influence. The other one was a GP but she had an ironclad alibi for the night in question. She was attending a home birth with a midwife. The child wasn't born until around dawn and they had been there all night while the woman was in labour. A regatta pundit, Sylvia Swann, drove a dark Mercedes, but at the time of the accident her car was in the carpark of a local radio station where she was giving a late-night interview."

"That's useful," said Horace. "What about Sir Andrew Eccles?"

"He was never questioned as far as I'm aware. The police said he was at home in Norfolk."

"You've been really helpful. Thank you."

"It's been years, but I also covered Michael Sebastian's drowning as he was a prominent local businessman. There didn't seem to be any red flags about his death, but now you mention it, he had been sniffing around asking questions about the hit-and-run. I didn't follow it up after he died because we had the regatta to cover with celebrities and royalty attending that year. Apart from the initial headline, it was relegated to the lesser-read pages."

"Do you know if Michael put anyone in particular's nose out of joint?"

"No, but there were hints that he'd got involved with drug dealers. He ran a pharmaceutical research company. You should speak to Sylvia Swann, his girlfriend at the time. She completely distanced herself from him before and after he died. I guess she didn't want mud sticking to her illustrious career, but I always felt she knew more than she let on.

"Anyway, I hope your friend makes a full recovery and you find out what happened. Check out the original police investigations, I think you'll find gaping holes in both. Rumour had it back in the day that one of the detectives was on the drug dealers' payroll and I wouldn't be surprised if Flame wasn't involved somewhere along that line."

Horace was scribbling fast into his notebook. *The only problem with that theory is that Stefan Flame is dead*, he thought. "Well, thanks again for your help."

"No problem. Give me your mobile number and I'll text you mine. You'll find it easier to get hold of me on that. I don't use the landline much and I'm out most days."

"Enjoying retirement?"

"Loving it. There's nothing like fresh sea air. The only issue down here is tourists, but we had plenty of them in Henley and I know all the out-of-the-way places now."

Horace read out his mobile number and received a text immediately. "Got it, thanks. Do you mind if I call you if anything else crops up?"

"Feel free, I've got plenty of time. Good luck," said Sharon. "It almost makes me want to get back in the game, but not really."

Horace sat back in the chair, thinking over what Sharon had said about the police investigation into the hit-and-run. Journalists could make things up and jump to conclusions to get a story, but in this case, she was retired so had no reason to. It appeared the incident had been hushed up and what the police had told Marjorie about the thorough investigation was not holding up.

That in itself was suspicious.

TWENTY-FOUR

After hearing the details of Horace's conversation with the retired journalist, Sharon Taylor, Marjorie was more convinced than ever that they were on the right track.

"Sharon's story is very different to that of DC Briar who told me the hit-and-run investigation was thorough and followed every lead."

"Yeah well, I wouldn't believe everything a journalist says, Marge. Remember, they make up the news as they go along. If it's not exciting enough they can't resist spicing it up."

"Ordinarily I would agree with you, Edna," said Horace, "but Sharon's retired and has no reason to embellish her story. If anything, she didn't get the chance to spice it up because her editor closed it down."

Marjorie scratched her head. "We're close and yet far from getting at the truth. Do we agree we can eliminate Reginald from the list of suspects?"

"I'm okay with that. From what the police told you, he wasn't in town on the night of the hit-and-run," said Horace.

"Neither was Andrew," said Edna.

"And Dr Christie was with a midwife and a birthing mother

all night. Sylvia Swann was giving a late-night radio interview, and yet I feel she knows more than she's saying about the days leading up to Michael's death. We're also running out of time. I suggest we go back to the regatta this morning and speak to Sylvia Swann again. If Michael was involved in drugs as Sharon implied, it's high time Ms Swann opened up about it."

Edna got up. "It's a start. Let's get going then. I want to catch the person who pushed Fred in the water and do the same to them."

Marjorie agreed with the sentiment.

"If it wasn't for the fact he's dead, I'd put my money on this Flame fellow. It sounds as though his business dealings were dirty and he was using the regatta as a cover," said Horace.

"I warned you about these posh people," said Edna folding her arms.

It wasn't worth arguing that corruption wasn't the exclusive remit of posh people, as Edna referred to them, and although the regatta linked the suspects, Marjorie doubted the place itself had any bearing on the crimes that had been committed. "Our priority is to find out who was driving the dark-coloured Mercedes on the night Michael's friend was killed. It's the key to everything."

"Well, it can't be that difficult to work it out if both Michael and Jonny knew who it was," said Horace.

"I don't believe Jonny knew. From what the police told me, he was casting his net wide, accusing everyone in the hope that someone would bite. Sadly, someone did, but not in the way he expected. Michael, however, I'm sure found out who it was. What I don't understand is why he didn't go straight to the police."

Horace donned his hat as they made their way out of the hotel. "Maybe Sharon was right and one of the cops was on a drug dealer's payroll. Or perhaps Michael wanted to confront the killer himself."

"But why attack Fred? It's not as if he'd found anything, was it?" asked Edna.

"I can only imagine the killer thought Jonny had imparted information that would lead him to them," said Marjorie.

"Or they are getting desperate," said Horace as they started their way down the path.

"Careless, I'd say," said Marjorie. "The fact the police are investigating Jonny Sebastian's death has unnerved them." Another thought came to her mind, but she didn't voice it just yet. It was something she wanted to mull over first.

The regatta was once again crowded, and the atmosphere was as exuberant as it had been throughout the week, but Marjorie's world had changed considerably. The fear she had felt over Frederick's near-death experience was overwhelming and the desire to find out who attacked him all-consuming. She was more determined than ever to get to the bottom of this mystery and judging by the steely looks on Horace and Edna's faces, they too were fully committed.

The problem was that the clock was ticking. The regatta had only two more days to run before life in Henley settled back to the way it had been before. Horace was flying to Bucharest to visit a cousin after the weekend, Edna had hospital appointments to attend, and Marjorie herself was flying to Iceland where she was joining a cruise from Reykjavik. There would be no-one to keep the investigation at the top of the police's list, and each suspect would return to their way of life. If that happened, someone would have got away with murder... again. The thought was intolerable.

"Are you all right, Marjorie?" Edna asked. The very fact she used Marjorie's full name meant she was concerned.

"I'm worried about Frederick, and concerned whoever did this to him might still get away with it."

"Not if we have anything to do with it, they won't."

Jostling through the larger crowds presented challenges. The event was gearing up to its conclusion.

Marjorie stopped for a moment. "It's not going to be easy to find people today. Edna, why don't you and Horace see if you can speak to Sir Andrew and ask what he was up to last night. Press him on his whereabouts on the night of the hit-and-run because I don't believe he was in Norfolk."

"Why?"

"Just a feeling, that's all. And even if he was, ask if he heard anything about the accident on the rumour mill. If Henley is anything, it's a place where people have theories. Someone knows something."

"We can also have another word with Oswald seeing as he's back in the picture, although I can't see him having the nerve to kill anyone. What are you going to do, Marjorie?" asked Horace.

"Speak to Sylvia Swann if I can. I'll try the press office and take it from there. I'd also like to have another word with Iris Flame in case her husband was involved in the hit-and-run."

"She seems pally with Andrew and quite protective of him, so if you don't get anywhere with Iris, Edna can persuade him to have a word on our behalf."

Marjorie smiled. "It's a shame to miss the racing today but my heart's not in it."

"First things first," said Edna. "Let's crack this case, and then we can think about posh people and their boats."

Marjorie appreciated the attempt at humour. Their friendship would see them through this tricky investigation. She suspected they might have to set a trap to find their killer and she wasn't afraid to put herself in harm's way to do it.

TWENTY-FIVE

Weaving her way through multitudes of happy people, Marjorie was aware her emotions were running high. But she was not one to put her feelings on display, and most people wouldn't have been able to see beyond the stoical mask she had on. That to her was a benefit. If she was going to tackle Michael Sebastian's ex-lover in a meaningful way, she would need to keep her feelings neutral. Edna was the complete opposite, but apart from rare occasions, Marjorie wouldn't want her cousin-in-law to be any different.

Each one of us has to be true to ourselves.

The energy drained from her legs as she found herself lost in the crowds. Being just over five feet tall could be an advantage when she wanted to listen in to conversations without being noticed, but this was not one of those occasions. Today, it was the exact opposite. She was searching for someone, and her height prevented her from seeing further than those in front of her. She needed to get to higher ground because, unlike Edna, who would most likely stand on a chair or do something equally ridiculous, Marjorie didn't have it in her nature to do so.

Thinking of Edna being outrageous brought a smile to her lips as Marjorie headed towards the grandstand.

Once there, Marjorie was able to scan the grounds below. Whilst she couldn't see inside the marquees, her eyes were able to pick out faces in the crowd. She caught sight of Iris Flame's distinctive pink suit and wondered what made a woman as wealthy as her always wear the same colour. Perhaps she should speak to Iris first. Whilst debating with herself, she looked over to speakers from where the commentary was booming through the grounds as the excitement of the latest race reached a crescendo.

"Go on, keep going!" Shouts came from the front row where a whole group of people dressed in a uniform edged forward in their seats, yelling at the top of their voices. The commentator was fuelling the excitement of what was turning out to be a close race between two boats surging towards the finishing line. Hysteria turned to disappointment as the whole row groaned in unison when their favourite was pipped at the finish line.

"At least they came second," a man tried to encourage his friends.

"Yes, but they should have won."

Marjorie had never felt the deep disappointment some experienced when watching sport. To her, it was always 'may the best team or person win', and even if she favoured one above another, it didn't affect her emotionally. Her son Jeremy would sulk for days if he was beaten at golf, or if his favourite cricket team lost. These were, in her opinion, wasted emotions. As her mind went back to how Frederick looked, lying in that hospital bed surrounded by monitors, waves of fear surged through her body and into her stomach.

She was once more focussed on the matter in hand. Iris Flame had disappeared from view. Marjorie caught sight of Edna's bright green hat and could just about make out her and

Horace speaking to Oswald Greene. At least they'd found their quarry.

Marjorie strained her eyes, trying to spot Sylvia Swann. It wasn't easy because she had only seen her once when Frederick pointed her out, but she had an excellent memory for faces. If only people didn't wear hats, she would have a better chance of spotting the woman's spiky grey hair.

"It's no use, you'll have to give up," she muttered.

The first aid tent was visible from Marjorie's vantage point and she could see Dr Christie having a heated conversation with the large man she and Frederick had seen her speaking to the day before. He was shifting crates around after checking inside each one. Dr Christie was patting him on the shoulder, but he shrugged her away. Whatever was going on between them, he was annoyed about it. Dr Christie leaned in closer to his face and said something before turning and marching towards the smoking area.

It was then that Marjorie spotted Sylvia Swann, who started chatting to the same man. He was equally gruff with Sylvia and turned his back on her, ignoring whatever it was she was saying.

Marjorie almost lost her footing on the steps as her knees gave way in her hurry to get down to where Sylvia was. A man put his hand out to catch her.

"Take it easy. These steps can be lethal," he said, tipping his hat after steadying her.

"Thank you," she muttered, then hurried in the direction of the woman in her sights.

By the time she got to where Sylvia Swann was standing outside of the first aid tent, the man had left. Sylvia was passing the time of day with numerous punters who all seemed to know her.

"Excuse me," Marjorie said. "Pardon me for interrupting, but might I have a word?"

The couple Sylvia was speaking to said their goodbyes and she peered down at Marjorie through intelligent and steely brown eyes. "What can I do for you?"

"You don't know me. My name is Marjorie Snellthorpe. You spoke to my friends Frederick Mackworth and Horace Tyler in St Mary's Church a few days ago and it's imperative I speak to you."

A frown crossed Sylvia's face.

"It really is important. You see, Frederick was attacked last night."

Sylvia's eyes widened. "Is he all right?"

"The doctors think he will make a full recovery, but... Look... is there somewhere quieter where we can talk?"

Sylvia hesitated before nodding. "Follow me."

Marjorie followed Sylvia into a prefabricated building that had been set up as offices for stewards and other officials. She greeted a slim man with long brown hair.

"I just need to use the back office for a few minutes. Is it free?"

"Anything for you, Sylvia. Go ahead." He smiled warmly at Marjorie.

Once the two women were seated in the tightly packed office, Sylvia looked at Marjorie. "I'm sorry about your friend, but I'm not sure I can help."

"I have to disagree. You know things about Michael Sebastian that might have a bearing on why he was killed. I'm not sure if Frederick told you, but he suspects his old friend Jonny Sebastian and Michael were both murdered. Why didn't you tell the police that you believed Michael was involved with drug dealers?"

Sylvia winced. "Where on earth did you get that information from? Whoever it was is quite wrong."

Marjorie held her ground. "Look, this is no longer about reputations, either yours or Michael's. This is about a person who has got away with murder. If you loved Michael Sebastian, it's time for some honesty. We are going to find this killer, but I need facts. No matter how hard it is for you."

Sylvia inhaled a deep breath before exhaling again. "All right. I suppose I've kept silent about this for long enough. You're right, Michael and I were having an affair. It was not as serious on his side, just one of those passionate diversions men who hit forty seem destined for, although he always had a roving eye."

"But from your side it was serious?" said Marjorie.

"Yes. Until I suspected he was trading in drugs. That took me by complete surprise because he hadn't ever hinted at such things."

"What made you believe he was involved in drug dealing?"

"We used to meet secretly in a pub on the outskirts of Henley. One day I arrived early. It was a beautiful summer's evening and I took a walk along the river before meeting Michael. On the way back from my walk, I noticed him sitting in one of those big SUVs with the windows blacked out. I wouldn't have seen him if he hadn't climbed out of the back of the vehicle about three hundred yards in front of me. The car sped off but I knew it didn't belong to anyone he normally associated with.

"When I arrived at the pub he was agitated and angry. Angrier than I'd ever seen him. I asked him what the matter was, but he snapped a reply. We argued, and when I mentioned seeing him get out of the SUV, he accused me of spying on him. He was lucky I didn't storm off, to be honest, but he calmed down and said it was nothing – just some private business. He wouldn't tell me who the person he'd met was, but warned me to have nothing to do with him. 'He's into some bad stuff,' was all he would say.

"I asked why he was meeting with him then, but he wouldn't give his reasons, just saying it was personal. When I made discreet enquiries, I found out the car belonged to a crooked local who hid behind a legitimate business, but I never discovered a name. I called Michael and told him I didn't want to see him anymore if he was taking or dealing in illicit drugs. He was livid and told me if that's what I thought about him, I could take a hike – or words to that effect."

"So, he denied being involved in drugs?" Marjorie asked.

"Well, he wasn't going to admit it, was he? I didn't want it to affect my job. I was starting to climb the ladder."

"And you felt you might be tainted by association?"

"Please understand, I loved him, but I never believed he loved me so the relationship was destined to end at some point. My career was all I had. When I heard about his death, it was devastating and took a long time to get over. Jonny's death brought it all back, which is why I was upset when your friends found me in the church."

"Did you believe the accidental drowning theory?" Marjorie held Sylvia's gaze. The other woman turned her head to stare through the window.

"All the evidence pointed that way, but I sometimes wondered if he'd decided to pull out of whatever it was he was doing and subsequently to end it all, or worse, that someone didn't like it."

"And yet you didn't mention any of this to the police?"

Sylvia swung her head in Marjorie's direction. "And lose my job, or end up dead myself? What good would that have done anyone? I'm sure you read the news. These people have a way of getting away with things."

"I don't believe Michael Sebastian was a drug dealer, or even a drug taker – apart from prescribed medication. He was trying to find out who was driving the car that killed his friend and employee, Casper Wolff."

Sylvia's eyes were wide and her jaw dropped open as she

considered what Marjorie had said. "Why wouldn't he tell me what he was doing?"

"Pride. Fear of getting you involved or looking a fool... Who knows?"

"So, you mean this person found out that Michael was trying to trace them and killed him?"

"Either that, or he did find out who was driving the car that night, challenged them, and they killed him. The end result was the same. If Jonny Sebastian was murdered, it makes perfect sense that so too was Michael, because Jonny was investigating Michael's death and had discovered the hit-and-run link."

"You'll excuse me if I find all this too difficult to take in. Things like that don't happen in Henley."

"So I keep hearing. And yet you have drug dealers and corrupt businessmen. I'm tired of being told what may or may not happen in Henley. In my world it's called burying your head in the sand."

Sylvia suddenly looked as though she had been struck, her bewildered eyes weighing everything up in an instant. "Could I have prevented Michael's death?"

"I doubt it," said Marjorie. "But if you had told the police about that meeting, you might have prevented other things, including Jonny's death."

"You think the man in the SUV killed Michael and Jonny?"

Marjorie massaged her temples. "I'm not sure, but they might know who did. Do you know who Michael spoke to?"

Sylvia shook her head. "I've always assumed it was Stefan Flame because of rumours about his illicit dealings and because he owned an SUV, but I didn't see him in the car, and if I'm honest, I didn't want to know. Now he's long dead."

"I understood Stefan Flame drove a dark Mercedes back then."

"He owned a Mercedes, but he almost always drove an

SUV – not that I can be certain that was the one Michael got out of that night. His wife Iris drove the Mercedes. I often saw her dropping the children off at school."

Marjorie's mind whirred with possibilities. "Is there anything else you can tell me?"

"Like what?"

"I don't know really. Anything Jonny or Michael said that might be relevant."

"Jonny had disagreements with everyone before he died: Iris, Elsa, Reginald, and Elsa's son."

"I haven't met Dr Christie's son but Frederick told me he's an Oxford graduate."

Sylvia burst out laughing, a cynical cackle. "He's no more of an Oxford graduate than I am. Elsa's in cloud-cuckoo-land as far as her son's concerned, but I don't blame her for that. She couldn't have children and paid privately for IVF treatment, but her obsession with having a child made her bitter. When Colin was born, she called him her little miracle, and after losing her husband when Colin was just twelve, she doted on him.

"Colin dropped out of Oxford and has lived at home ever since. He's surly like his mother and doesn't have any friends. You might see him lugging crates around by the first aid tent. Those two are always arguing these days. Elsa should have cut him loose years ago then she might have reason to be proud of him. But that's just my opinion and a lot of it is from observation. Elsa Christie and I aren't friends."

"Then how do you know all this?"

"Michael was in and out of the surgery where Elsa worked. Before she got pregnant, she made a lot of people's lives hell and the staff would warn him when to steer clear. Look, I'd better get back now. I said I'd advise the commentators on the next few races. They're new and don't have the background."

Marjorie mused for a while after Sylvia left the cramped office. Every time she thought they were getting closer to the truth, more curveballs were thrown their way.

TWENTY-SIX

It was easy to track down Oswald Greene. Horace found him hanging around the boat sheds.

"Do you mind if we ask you a few more questions?"

Oswald scowled. "I've told you everything I know and I'd appreciate being left alone. Andrew has been released and now I know Michael's death had nothing to do with me."

"Ooh, touchy," said Edna. "But you haven't told us everything, have you? You didn't mention that you drove a dark Mercedes when Michael's friend Casper was mown down like a piece of litter and left to die in the road."

Oswald's eyes almost popped out of his head. "I don't believe you people! What's the matter with you? First you tell me I didn't kill Michael, and now you're accusing me of God knows what!"

Horace spoke in a calm, determined voice. "We're just trying to establish the facts. You did drive a dark Mercedes twenty-two years ago?"

"Me and thousands of others in Henley – and all over the country, for that matter."

"It was an odd omission considering we told you Michael was looking into the death of his friend," said Edna.

Oswald looked baffled. "What's my car got to do with anything? Besides, at the time, I was relieved to find it wasn't pressure on Michael from me that caused him to kill himself. And no matter what you nosey parkers say, I still think he drowned by accident. Andrew told me the police think Jonny took his own life after sedating himself."

"Oh, really, Mr Clever Clogs," said Edna. "I think you'll find the police are revising that theory after our friend Frederick was almost killed last night."

Oswald barely flinched at the news.

"You already know about that," said Horace.

"Word gets around. I suppose you're going to pin that one on me as well."

"You've changed your tune, Mister," said Edna. "Yesterday you were racked with guilt, now you're the innocent party who knows nothing about nobody."

The sweat on Oswald's forehead suggested Edna was getting through.

"I've had a bad day and just want to be left alone." Oswald's tone was sullen.

"Not half as bad as we have," said Edna, not backing off. "Our friend is lying in a hospital bed having almost died last night so I doubt your petty little problems are anything by comparison. And don't tell me it's because you lost a stupid race or something."

"Worse than that. I've been told my services are no longer required here. I might not have been responsible for Michael Sebastian's death, but word's got around I'm a bully. This is my last day as a volunteer advisor."

Edna was about to blow a gasket but Horace intervened.

"Sorry to hear that. I've seen how important the regatta... and rowing... is to you. If you could just clarify what you told the police when they interviewed you after the hit-and-run accident, we'll be on our way."

"And you can lick your wounds," muttered Edna under her breath.

"I don't know what you're talking about. No-one interviewed me about any such thing."

Horace rubbed his forehead. "Are you sure? We were told the police interviewed you and several others about your whereabouts following Casper Wolff's death."

Oswald shook his head. "I'm telling you, nobody asked me about that. Are you saying a Mercedes was involved in that accident?"

Edna tutted. "Doh! Yes. A dark Mercedes."

"I owned a black Mercedes back then, but I hardly ever drove it. There wasn't much need for driving in Henley, and I used the boat to cross the river from my house, then walked."

"You must have used it to go to other races. What about Marlow, Oxford, Cambridge, and Reading?" Horace said.

"Only if I wasn't towing boats."

"You must remember the night that man was killed," said Edna. "What were you doing then?"

"Okay, I admit Jonny asked me the same question and I told him the same as I'll tell you. Back then, I travelled a lot. I must have been out of town because I don't remember the event at all."

"I find that hard to believe," said Edna. "After all, how many hit-and-runs do you have in Henley?"

"It didn't happen in Henley; it was on the Reading Road."

Gotcha! Edna thought. "So you do remember?"

"Come on, Oswald. It's time to tell the truth, if only to clear yourself."

"Okay, okay. I was so busy with work and coaching, I'd inadvertently let the tax and insurance lapse on the car. The investigating sergeant was a friend from the rowing club. He took a look at my car just to eliminate it from his enquiries and told me not to forget to sort out my documentation in future. We left it at that."

Edna felt her throat tighten as she struggled to contain her emotions. Anger was never too far from the surface these days and nothing riled her more than people in power or with connections abusing their position.

"Just to clarify," said Horace, taking Edna's hand, "you didn't drive your car on the night of the hit-and-run, and the police sergeant did inspect your car for signs of damage?"

Oswald avoided Edna's eyes and answered Horace in a milder tone than he had used thus far. "Marty told me the car that hit the person would have a damaged headlight. They found glass at the scene. He also said there would be blood and tissue traces on the bonnet. Apparently, the driver didn't slow down before or after the collision. There were no skid marks at the scene."

"And you didn't take your car to the garage in the days following the accident?" Edna's eyes narrowed as she looked at him.

"Not until after Marty had checked it. It erm... also needed an MOT."

"What kind of—"

Horace took Edna's arm, leading her away from Oswald Greene. "I know what you were going to say, but his neglecting to get a compulsory motor test years ago, is not going to help now. We need to concentrate our energies on who was driving on the night of the hit-and-run, and who pushed Fred into the river last night."

"You're not buying that nonsense, are you?"

"Actually, I am. He was an arrogant idiot back in the day, but I believe his story. What we need to find out is whether this Sergeant Marty whatever-his-name-was let anything else go. If we need to go back over Oswald's story, we can tell DS Cramer. For now, we rule him out."

"Shame you can't prosecute for past motoring offences, but I doubt his mate even kept notes after the interview. Now what?"

Horace checked his watch. "Time for lunch. We'll exchange information with Marjorie and plan our next course of action. We can also get an update on Fred."

Edna patted her stomach. "All that talk of blood and tissue is enough to put me off food, but I'm surprisingly hungry."

"That's my girl," said Horace, patting her on the shoulder. "Well done back there, you did bad cop very well."

Edna didn't like to admit she wasn't trying to play bad anything, she was just plain annoyed with the likes of Oswald Greene and his attitude. "At least he's lost his place in this particular society. Nothing more than he deserves."

"Now, now, Edna, don't be so quick to judge. We've all made errors of judgement in the past."

"Yeah, and you more than most," said Edna chortling.

TWENTY-SEVEN

Over lunch, Marjorie listened to Horace and Edna's revelations about what Oswald Greene had to confess. She wasn't happy that the historic enquiry into the hit-and-run accident was nowhere near as thorough as DC Briar believed. She planned to tell him or Sergeant Cramer so when she next spoke to one of them.

"I take it you believe Oswald is telling the truth?"

Edna had been angry when she and Horace shared their discovery and, on this occasion, Marjorie couldn't blame her.

"I suppose so, although it took him a while to come out with it," said Edna. "I doubt he would have concocted such a story. If he was going to lie, he'd have come up with something better."

"I agree," said Horace. "I didn't have him down as a killer anyway. He was overwhelmed by the guilt he'd been carrying around for decades."

"Not having tax or insurance would give a person reason to drive away from the scene of an accident. But then he wouldn't bring it out in the open now, so I'm inclined to agree with you and rule him out."

"What did you find out, Marge?"

"First of all, I contacted the hospital and they let me speak to Frederick. He's insisting on being discharged today although the doctors and his son would like him to stay for another day. Alas, he didn't see his attacker and doesn't remember anything after being pushed into the water. The fisherman has been to visit him and couldn't help because he saw nothing but a shadow, which is all that Frederick saw."

"Did he say why he went tearing off into the night on his own?" Edna asked.

"Just that he received a text from someone saying they had important information and were about to leave Henley. He assumed it was from Sharon Taylor, not having her mobile phone number. As we know, he gave many people his number, and whoever sent the message did so anonymously. Frederick's phone hasn't been recovered and sending in divers isn't a priority."

"I'd like to know what the police around here do see as a priority."

"That's not fair, Edna," Horace interjected. "They have to police the regatta, which I'm sure comes with a significant burden on their resources."

"Similar to football matches I suppose," said Marjorie. "Anyway, Frederick has spoken to DS Cramer and explained what happened from his perspective. I'd like to speak to the sergeant or DC Briar and let them know the earlier investigation into the hit-and-run accident wasn't as good as they thought. Certainly not as thorough as they led me to believe... which brings me on to Sylvia Swann."

"What did lover-girl have to say?" Edna raised an eyebrow.

"She was convinced Michael had got in with a bad lot after seeing him getting out of an SUV one night when she was due to meet him. He was cagey about the meeting, and wouldn't tell her what it was about, or who he met. The interesting thing is she thought it was a so-called respectable businessman who conducted murky business on the side. She believed drugs."

"Was this man Stefan Flame by any chance?" Horace asked.

"She thought so. What made you think of him?" Marjorie said.

"I've been asking around and a lot of people suggest he built his empire on dubious foundations. They mentioned money laundering, betting scandals and payoffs, so drugs wouldn't be beyond the realms of possibility."

"Well, the really interesting thing I discovered was that his wife, Iris, drove the Mercedes, although it was registered in his name."

"And I doubt the cops wanted to bother this pillar of society by checking his or his wife's alibi," said Edna.

"I expect if they did any checking at all, it was low-key like Oswald Greene's," said Marjorie. "That's for the current police to check.

"But it puts Iris Flame in the frame, doesn't it?" Edna said.

"It might explain why she was so upset when Sir Andrew was arrested," said Marjorie. "If it hadn't been for the attack on Frederick last night, the police were going back to the suicide theory. The killer has overplayed their hand."

Horace cut into his steak dinner. "That's good in a way, it shows they're getting desperate."

"And bad in another way because they're dangerous. I'd rather Frederick remain in the safety of the hospital ward with a police guard, but he sounded determined. He's worried one of us might come to harm."

Edna polished off the lamb on her plate, swilling the last mouthful down with a gulp of water. "Which could happen, Marge. I bet we're all in the killer's sights."

Marjorie chuckled. "That's what I'm hoping."

"I'd like to point out that this isn't a game. Fred nearly died last night."

"I know that, Edna, so I'm proposing we lay a trap the killer can't resist."

Edna wiped her mouth with a napkin before pulling out a makeup mirror and retouching her lipstick. Satisfied all was back as it should be, she stared at Marjorie.

"I hate it when you say things like that. It always means danger. I'm telling you now, I won't be bait for no psychopath."

"Don't worry, Edna, you won't be the bait. I will."

Edna puffed her cheeks, staring desperately at Horace. "Talk some sense into her, will you? She's likely to end up dead."

Horace's forehead wrinkled into thin lines of concentration. "I think we should save any such plan as a last resort, Marjorie. If the police don't get to the bottom of it soon, we'll hear you out."

Marjorie said nothing, but she was already hatching a plan in her head because she was convinced it was the only way to draw this wily killer into the open.

"Did Sylvia say anything else of use?" Horace asked.

"Not really. She felt guilty over Michael's death, but she'll go back into her shell of denial. Although she admitted her career came first, we've managed to catch her at moments of vulnerability. I doubt she would be easily persuaded to display her weakness again."

"What about Dr Christie? Frederick seemed to think she could be helpful. As a GP, she must have heard things, and it was she who called the police about Michael's death. I wonder if she saw the hit-and-run victim," said Horace.

"No. The man was dead and would have been taken straight to the hospital. In all honesty, I don't think she had any intention of helping Frederick at all. She strikes me as someone who wants to stay under the radar now she's retired. Quite an eccentric woman who's not afraid to offend people."

Horace steepled his hands beneath his chin. "I'd still like to have a go at her myself. I might be able to put on the old charm. Is she widowed?"

"You're such a flirt, Horace Tyler," said Edna.

"One thing Sylvia said was that Dr Christie's son isn't a graduate of Oxford. I was sure Frederick mentioned how proud she was of him but Sylvia believes the doctor's blind where her son is concerned."

"She wouldn't be the first parent to want to exaggerate her child's achievements, although why lie about it?"

Marjorie thought of her own son, Jeremy. Although he ran her late husband's company, it remained successful in spite of him, rather than because of him. Others did the hard work and Marjorie kept hold of the business's purse strings, being a partner with controlling interest. Would she lie about his achievements? Perhaps not, but she covered for him often enough.

"I don't suppose it's anything. But if you do speak to her, Horace, ask her about him in case Frederick was mistaken."

"Is it relevant?" said Edna.

"I doubt it, but if she's capable of lying about something like that, who knows what else she isn't saying?"

"Good point, Marjorie," said Horace. "If she'll speak to me, I'll try to work it into the conversation."

"So, what's next?" Edna asked.

"Before speaking to Dr Christie, Horace could speak to Sharon Taylor again and ask whether she did any investigative work off the record, particularly looking into cars and alibis. Edna, we'll try Iris Flame."

The Luncheon Tent was filling up and getting rowdy. Somehow the joyous laughter that had been so infectious earlier in the week rang hollow in Marjorie's head. Her concentration was no longer on the regatta, but was consumed with thoughts about a deadly killer wandering around the place as if nothing had happened. Whoever they were looking for had no conscience whatsoever and she was determined to see them in prison where they belonged, even if she had to set the trap by herself.

TWENTY-EIGHT

Edna had loved the regatta's atmosphere far more than she'd expected to. Watching the races and chatting to friendly people in between their side hustle had given her more pleasure than she'd felt in a long time. If only Fred hadn't run into his old friend, they wouldn't be in this predicament. The only way to get Marge and Horace back into the sunny frame of mind they had started out with was to get to the bottom of the mystery that had plagued lives for decades.

With only a day and a half to go, despite what she'd said over lunch, she was going to draw this killer out so they could return to some sense of normality. Besides that, she didn't want Marge putting herself in danger. Edna suspected her cousin would do just that. Studying Marge's eyes over lunch, she had sensed it. Her friends might tease her about never listening, but she could read Marge more than she thought.

Edna had excused herself after lunch, saying she was suffering a headache after the disturbed night – true – and that she was going back to the hotel for a lie down – not true. Instead, she hovered outside the Fawley Bar until she saw who she was looking for.

Sir Andy beamed when he caught sight of her. "Edna! How nice to see you again. The lime green suits you just as much as the yellow."

She grinned. "For someone who's been arrested and released, you're very chipper."

"That was rather unfortunate. Was it you and your friends who got me off the hook?"

Edna shook her head. "Sorry. Although we believed you were innocent, it wasn't our doing. Did you hear Fred was attacked last night?"

"No, I didn't. After spending yesterday in the discomfort of the local nick, I went out for a slap-up meal and had a lie in this morning. Is he okay?"

"He will be."

"Can I buy you a drink?"

"I wouldn't say no to some more of that pink champagne," said Edna.

"Then come along, fair lady. Have you done something to your hair? It looks different."

Edna had donned her favourite red wig this morning for a change from the black bob. "It's a long story," she answered.

Andrew took her reply in his stride, not pressing the issue. Once they were seated with a bottle of pink champagne and two glasses, he locked eyes with her. He was stunningly attractive despite his age, but that wasn't foremost on her mind right now.

"Do the police know who attacked your friend?"

"Not yet, but I do."

"Oh? Do tell."

Edna tapped her nose. "For now, I'm keeping it to myself. I'll be speaking to the police later today."

Andrew clinked her glass with his. "To justice and my freedom," he said.

"Cheers," she replied.

"If you do know whodunnit, don't you think you should get on and tell the police? I wouldn't like to spend another day being quizzed by the boys and girls in blue."

"The thing is, I still need a few more facts before I can be certain."

Andrew's shoulders sagged. His eyes looked tired with heavy dark bags underneath. "Did this person kill Jonny Sebastian?"

Edna nodded. "And Michael, and a man called Casper Wolff."

"Good heavens! A serial killer."

"Not in the usual definition of the psycho type, but this person is a psychopath in every other sense. They kill without remorse."

"Is there anything I can do to help?"

"You can start by telling me what you've heard on the Henley grapevine. There might be some evidence in there that will help me put the final pieces of the jigsaw together."

Andrew finished his champagne and refilled his glass. Edna was taking it slow. She would need her wits about her if she was to draw the killer into the open – the murderer she in reality had no clue about.

"Although I have a house in Henley I'm not kept in the loop as far as the latest gossip is concerned. I only visit once a year nowadays and my nephew uses the house to entertain business guests... or so he says." Andrew winked. "But I'm assuming you're referring to the period a couple of decades ago when I spent a lot more time here?"

"Yep. You've hit the nail on the head."

Andrew looked over his shoulder, checking they weren't being listened to. Edna doubted his logic. How would he know when the tent was jam-packed?

"I heard about the hit-and-run people are mentioning because I was in Henley at the time it happened. In fact, I voluntarily told a detective friend of mine that I drove a black Mercedes."

Edna raised a quizzical eyebrow. "And?"

"And nothing. He accepted my word that I was home all evening."

"Did he look at the car?"

Andrew shook his head. "No. He trusted me and he was right to. I was nowhere near the scene of the crime."

"But the police told Marge you weren't interviewed because you were in Norfolk at the time. Surely he would have taken a statement?" Edna was becoming less and less impressed with the original investigation.

"Actually, he didn't. I asked for his discretion, although I didn't ask him to say I was in Norfolk. You see – and I'm not proud of this, Edna – but I was with a woman and I didn't want my wife or – more importantly – the lady's husband to hear about it."

"What woman?"

"Er" – Andrew cleared his throat – "Iris Flame."

Edna felt as if her head was going to explode. "The woman in pink? Seriously?"

"We had a short and not so exciting fling. Her heart wasn't in it."

"Why?"

"She still loved her husband. It was perhaps as well, because Stefan Flame was a nasty piece of work and if he'd ever found out about our little affair, I'd have been toast."

"Did she stay all night?"

"Her husband was away, but she left at around five to relieve the nanny and take the kids to school."

Edna tried to calculate the timings with what she knew about the hit-and-run accident. If Andrew was telling the truth, they had joint alibis. However, if he was lying, neither had an alibi and they were covering each other.

"You do know she drove her husband's dark Mercedes?" Edna said.

"She was with me, Edna."

"Hmm. What else did your copper friend tell you?"

"He admitted to believing the driver was a local, but he wasn't in charge of the investigation, and he thought the inspector could have been in Flame's pocket."

"And Stefan Flame wanted it covered up?"

"You're going to jump to conclusions, but I might as well tell you because I know Iris is innocent. On the way home, she hit a bollard and broke a headlight. As neither of us could tell Stefan what had really happened, she had to lie about the time, and he put pressure on the inspector to shift the enquiry elsewhere."

"To an out-of-towner?"

"Precisely. Iris told her husband the prang had happened much earlier than it had because she didn't want him to ask why she was out in the early hours, although she didn't realise she would need an alibi... or a cover story for why the car went for repairs. Stefan took it to an Oxford garage and no more was said about the incident."

"Do you think he believed she had run over and killed Casper Wolff?"

"He might well have done, but he never mentioned it to Iris again. She was terrified when I was arrested yesterday. She thought I'd tell the police what had happened and she might be arrested too."

"Or lose her good name as the grieving benefactor of numerous charities?"

"Possibly a bit of that too."

"Did your copper friend know who you were with and about her accident?"

"No. He was an honest chap. That would have been a step

too far. He just trusted me when I said I was at home with a woman."

Edna blew out an exasperated sigh. "I'll never understand why you men can't stay faithful to one woman."

"She was married too, Edna. You see, I believe her story, but I never knew what time she left my house. I was blotto."

Idiot, thought Edna. "Anything else you're not telling me?"

"There is something else, but I don't think it's relevant."

"Tell me anyway if you want your old flame—" She winked.

"Very funny."

"—not to be in police custody by the end of the day."

As Edna listened to what Andrew had to say, she felt her heart miss several beats. Could this be the breakthrough they were looking for? Suddenly, her phone sent her handbag into a jumping frenzy. It really was time to ask Horace to take a look at the vibrate function and make it less harsh.

"You get that, I'll get us another bottle."

Us? You've drunk almost the whole bottle, she thought. Obviously baring one's soul required liquid nourishment. Edna pulled the phone from her handbag and listened to her voicemail. It was Horace.

"Where are you? I'm back at the hotel and Dinah says you never returned. Please contact me asap! I'm worried."

Edna sent a text:

> On my way.

She finished the glass of champagne she'd been resisting, before waving to the astonished Andrew Eccles on her way out of the tent. He sent a 'so be it' wave back and started gassing to a few animated punters who were sharing a jug of Pimm's as though their lives depended on it.

TWENTY-NINE

Marjorie was for once carrying her mobile phone, and because she was taking a walk near to the boathouses, having given up her mission of tracking down Iris Flame with the crowds growing rather than shrinking, she heard it ring.

Twenty minutes later, Marjorie was back at the hotel.

The sitting room was sweltering and the gas fire was lit despite the temperature outside rising again to twenty-three degrees. After the brief respite the night before, the heatwave Henley was experiencing showed no signs of disappearing.

"I'm pleased to see you, but are you sure you should be out of hospital?" Not being a hugger, Marjorie pecked Frederick on the cheek.

His face flushed. "The doctor gave me a clean bill of health and told me that as long as I stay indoors in the warm, I could go home."

"That explains why we're sitting in an oven," said Edna. "Some people will do anything to get attention." Although Edna's words were sharp, her tone suggested she was just as pleased to see Frederick as the rest of them.

"How are you really?" Marjorie asked him.

"Tired but, all things considered, I'm doing fine," said Frederick.

"Well in that case, it's time for a catchup. I take it you still haven't remembered anything else about last night?"

Frederick shook his head. "Sorry. I never should have gone on my own, I know that now."

Edna opened her mouth to say something but Horace gave her a gentle nudge.

"Have the others told you I had a rather enlightening conversation with Sylvia Swann?" said Marjorie. "Actually enlightening might be an exaggeration. She, as you know, was having an affair with Michael Sebastian. It ended after she saw him in a car with a person she presumed was dealing in drugs. It was an SUV and Sylvia believed, but can't be certain, that it belonged to Stefan Flame."

"Apparently it was his wife who drove the Mercedes," said Horace. "Edna and I filled Frederick in on the details of your conversation with the detectives last night, Marjorie, so he knows the suspects who drove cars which could have been involved in the hit-and-run."

Edna was bouncing up and down, agitated. "I've got more to add to that, Marge. I had another chat with Andrew."

"While you were supposedly here having a lie down," said Horace.

"Sorry, but what I found out is really important. Andrew was in Henley on the night of the hit-and-run—"

"I knew it was him," Frederick snapped, glaring.

"Hold your horses, mate... there's more," said Edna, shifting impatiently in her seat, but drawing the moment out.

"When you're quite ready," said Marjorie.

"He was with Iris Flame."

Stunned silence filled the room while Edna kept them waiting for more information.

"Not only that, but she had an accident on the way home that night and damaged her headlamp."

"Why wasn't Sir Andrew interviewed?" Marjorie asked.

"He had a mate in the police and asked him to be discreet. The mate checked his car for damage and left it at that. Andrew didn't know the detective was going to fabricate his whereabouts, but he and Iris were frightened of Stefan Flame finding out."

"Did Iris tell the police about her accident?"

"No. Andrew swears he was with her until the early hours, although he says he was blotto and can't be certain she left at five, which is when she told him she left. Her story was that she hit a bollard. She told her husband about the accident, but didn't dare tell him about the time it happened. Andrew says Flame had one of the senior detectives on his payroll and the car was never checked."

"But now we know that Sir Andrew was in Henley on the night of the hit-and-run," said Frederick. "I still reckon it was him."

"And I still disagree. Andrew's car was checked."

Marjorie wondered why Edna wasn't shortening Sir Andrew's name to Andy, something she would normally do. After the initial few days of calling him names, she'd changed her tune to being far more positive.

"But we only have his word for it, because presumably his police officer friend didn't record the interview," she said.

Edna folded her arms across her chest. "Well, I believe him. It makes sense. Neither he nor Iris could afford to let her husband find out. He was dangerous."

"What if they were both in Iris's car?" Horace quizzed. "And they're covering for each other."

"That's the best theory I've heard so far," said Frederick. "Not to mention he hangs about the river when bodies are found. I bet it was him who pushed me in the river last night."

"He didn't," said Edna, raising her voice and glaring around the room.

"Edna," said Marjorie, gently, "I realise you like Sir Andrew, but we must keep an open mind about what happened. We can't believe everything he says."

"I accept Iris might have left earlier than he thought she did and that she could have been driving the Mercedes responsible for the hit-and-run, but you have to hear the rest of what I found out before jumping to conclusions."

As it was normally Edna jumping to conclusions, Marjorie felt slightly irritated, but there was no point having an argument. "Then please enlighten us. What else do you know?"

They listened intently as Edna shared the rest of what Sir Andrew had told her, and Marjorie had to admit, it was an avenue she hadn't even considered.

Frederick's eyes changed from tired to angry. "He could just be spinning you more lies to shift the blame away from him. Remember, it was him the police had reason to arrest," he said.

"You really have got it in for him, haven't you?" said Edna. "Why?"

Frederick spluttered before peering down at his trembling hands. "Because I believe he killed Jonny."

Marjorie shot Edna a warning look before taking Frederick's hand in hers. "If he did, we'll prove it. Please don't exert yourself, you've been through an awful experience. It's important we check Sir Andrew's story."

"There's no harm in following both lines of enquiry but before we do, I think we should call the police," said Horace.

"And fast!" Edna said.

Horace left the room to make the phone call while Marjorie ensured Frederick ate and drank something. They talked about the hospital and the nurses. Marjorie asked him how his son was. Anything to take his mind off of the events that filled all their heads.

When Horace returned, he shook his head. "The desk person said the detectives are busy at the moment. I've left a message."

"Then we have work to do," said Marjorie, not prepared to delay when her friend had a target on his back. "I suggest you make a few phone calls and then find me. We'll know who our killer is by the end of play today." Marjorie scribbled some notes down on a pad and handed it to Horace.

"I'm coming with you," said Frederick.

"But you're supposed to stay in the warm..." One look at Frederick's unusually set jaw told Marjorie arguments would be pointless, and besides, there wasn't a moment to lose. "All right. As long as Edna is with you the whole time and you both hang back when I find Iris or Dr Christie."

"Fine," he said, getting up. He wobbled and Marjorie almost changed her mind.

"Don't worry, Marge. I'll take care of him."

Marjorie acquiesced, wanting to get on with things.

THIRTY

Marjorie had been wandering around the regatta while Horace made some phone calls. Edna and Frederick were keeping their distance. Just as Marjorie was passing the grandstand, Dr Christie stopped her.

"I've been looking for you," the former doctor said. Despite being in the non-smoking part of the enclosure, she had a burning cigarette in her right hand. Frederick had said she was not one to believe that rules applied to her. She took a couple of puffs, blowing smoke into the air as if daring anyone to challenge her. Apart from a few disapproving looks and turned-up noses, nobody did.

"Really? Why?"

"I heard your friend Frederick's in a coma."

"Not anymore," said Marjorie. "He's conscious and insisting on discharging himself." Marjorie didn't want anyone to know Frederick was out of hospital until she was sure he would be safe.

"That's never a good idea. Silly man might go into shock."

"Try telling him that. I'm still hoping he'll listen to the doctors and to reason."

"To be honest, I wasn't sold on the whole suspicious deaths theory, but after hearing he was attacked, I'm having my doubts. He was attacked, wasn't he?"

"He received a mysterious text message from a person claiming to have knowledge of the hit-and-run. Whoever sent it lured him to the same part of the river where Jonny and Michael Sebastian died."

"So it's true. I wondered if it was just gossip and he'd become depressed about Jonny's death. He seemed the morose type."

"Frederick may be serious but he's not depressed. He was most certainly pushed into the river by a deranged individual."

Dr Christie threw her cigarette butt to the floor and stamped it into the ground. At any other time, Marjorie would have insisted she pick it up, but after a quick check to see it was fully extinguished, she made to walk away.

"Perhaps I can help persuade your friend to stay in hospital."

"Would you? I didn't think you were interested before. We are very close to finding out who the killer is, and that would be a huge weight off my mind."

"I've been thinking about all that you both said. It's Iris Flame, isn't it?"

"What makes you think it was her?"

"Normally I wouldn't say anything because of doctor-patient confidentiality, but I draw the line at murder. I treated Iris for depression for years. Her husband was a bully, and she was afraid of him and his shady dealings."

"That fits with what Sylvia Swann told me."

A look of surprise crossed Dr Christie's face. "She knew as well, did she?"

"Guessed rather than knew for certain, I would say. Please continue."

"It's not common knowledge, but Iris Flame and Sir

Andrew Eccles were having an affair back then. Iris was distraught when she came to see me because she'd hit something on the road on the night of the hit-and-run. This was about six months after the event. She thought it was a bollard, but was too scared to tell her husband where she'd been because she was with Andrew and had been drinking."

"And you believed her?"

"There was no reason not to at the time. She was terrified of her husband. It happened on a Thursday night, or rather in the early hours of Friday morning. She drove to another town or city to have the headlamp repaired. In view of recent events, I've wrestled with my conscience about it and have been to the police."

"So, her husband didn't know anything about this accident?" This was a different story to that Sir Andrew had told Edna.

"Not unless she told him later. When he was diagnosed with cancer, he was a much weakened man, and Iris became the strong one. I should have realised how manipulative she could be. She played the loving wife to extremes and ensured that all his money was left to her. Even I was taken in. I'm sure that when the police question her and Sir Andrew, they'll admit to giving each other alibis that night."

"I see," said Marjorie trying to process what she was hearing. "I must admit I was leaning in another direction entirely, but what do I know?"

"What direction was that?"

Marjorie saw Horace over Dr Christie's shoulder. He nodded, giving her a thumbs up.

"I don't suppose it matters now, but I thought you might be involved."

Dr Christie cackled. "You need to get your facts straight. I was with a woman who had an interminably long labour that night. I wouldn't normally have stayed that long but she was a colleague's daughter. The infant was born at six o'clock the next morning."

"I know where you were on the night of the hit-and-run, but you didn't drive there, did you?" Marjorie said.

"Pardon?"

"The midwife drove."

"Did she? I don't recall. Whoever drove, I was not on the Reading Road."

"Oh, I think you do recall who was driving your dark Mercedes on that night. I understand your son often used your car. It was he who knocked that poor man over."

"Don't be ridiculous! That's the most absurd story I've ever heard. My son was at Oxford University in halls."

Horace joined the conversation at this point, appearing from behind Dr Christie, who lit up another cigarette with trembling hands. "From what I understand, your son had a row with his girlfriend that night and was driving home to Mummy in a state. Tears and stress affected his vision and he drove into a man walking along the Reading Road. He didn't even stop to call an ambulance."

Dr Christie's eyes were darting around as what Horace had said registered with her. She leaned in closer to Horace, glaring.

"That's a lie. My son was at Oxford and he had his own car at that time."

Edna joined them at that moment with Frederick. Dr Christie stared wide-eyed at Frederick's presence.

"His car was in the garage. You hardly used yours and he'd borrowed it for the week. When he told you what had happened, you covered for him. The next day he wanted to go to the police, but you persuaded him not to," said Edna, her voice dribbling with sarcasm. "After all, who's going to doubt a reputable doctor?"

"You didn't want him to lose his place at Oxford University. You told him it was a simple error of judgement," said Frederick. "You were a doctor! You've broken every vow you ever took to save and to preserve life. Instead, you covered up a fatal road traffic accident which carried a minimal prison sentence back then and murdered two people in order to keep your secret. You nearly got me too, but you don't realise that wouldn't have stopped my friends from tracking you down with every last breath."

Marjorie enjoyed hearing Frederick bringing this woman down a peg. "No wonder your son dropped out of university," she said. "Despite your evil efforts."

"He knows what you've done, by the way. Something he suspected, but you denied," said Edna.

"That man was already dead," Dr Christie snapped. "My son had his whole life in front of him. After going to all that trouble to keep him out of prison, I wasn't going to let Michael Sebastian ruin his life."

"Why do I think there's more to this story than you're telling us?" Marjorie said.

Dr Christie's head dropped. "Stefan Flame found out what had happened. His wife had told him about her accident so he hired a private investigator to check all the cars. Afterwards, the blackmail started. He got me to prescribe opiates for non-existent patients. I didn't want to do it, but I had no choice."

"We always have a choice," said Marjorie.

"As well as being a regular at our surgery, Michael visited a lot of the pharmacies in his research capacity, and over time he put two-and-two together. He met Stefan, who tried to warn him off. Not long afterwards, he came to see me and told me he was giving me the opportunity to hand my son in to the police, or he would do it himself. But can't you see? There was more at stake than my son's mistake by that time; my whole career was on the line. I'd have been struck off."

That's why Michael and Stefan Flame had a falling out, thought Marjorie.

"So, you found out about his meeting with Sir Andrew, drugged him and pushed him in the Thames," said Edna, disgusted.

"He was surprised to see me. I pleaded with him not to take the matter any further but he said his friend deserved justice. Even when I told him what would happen to me, he said that was my fault. I did what I had to do to protect my son and what any mother would have done," Dr Christie snapped.

"I don't think so," said Marjorie. "I'm a mother and I would have accompanied my son to the police station."

"And as a father, so would I," said Frederick.

"Hear, hear," said Horace.

"Then none of you know what it's like to love your child. I mean, really love your child."

"Suffocate more like," Edna snapped. "Do you have any idea what you've done? You snuffed out two lives and tried to take another. You're a pathetic human being who's going to jail, along with your pathetic son! You might have saved your own neck before, but you won't this time."

Dr Christie blew smoke in Edna's face, stretching to her full height. "You forget, I've given the police my statement and I've been a respected member of the community for over forty years. I think you'll find they'll take my word over yours. They have taken Iris Flame in for questioning. You have nothing on me. I suggest you get out of my way. Now!" Dr Christie attempted to barge past, but Edna's larger frame blocked her.

"Not so fast, Missus. I believe the sergeant would like a word before you go anywhere."

Marjorie was as surprised as Dr Christie to see Sergeant Cramer and DC Briar appear.

Frederick leaned in and whispered, "We didn't get the chance to tell you. DC Briar called while you were talking to Dr Christie, and after I explained what Andrew had told Edna, we suggested the police come straight down, but he said they already knew."

"Dr Elsa Christie, I'm arresting you for the murder of Jonathan Sebastian, the suspected murder of Michael Sebastian, the attempted murder of Frederick Mackworth and for concealing a crime leading to a death by dangerous driving. DC Briar will read you your rights."

DC Briar did as asked, then said, "Please come with us."

"I've told you everything I know. Iris Flame is responsible for the historic hit-and-run case and most likely killed the Sebastians to keep them quiet."

"We have your son, Colin, at the station. He's given us a full statement. And Mrs Flame uncovered evidence of historic blackmail from her husband's meticulous notes. Something she wasn't aware of until recently as they were hidden under the false bottom of a desk drawer."

All colour drained from Dr Christie's face, then her eyes blazed with fire. She fixed them on Marjorie. "You think you're so clever, don't you? Well, let me tell you now, I'm cleverer, and you'll pay for this. You and all your friends."

"I'm afraid while you're languishing in prison, Dr Christie," said Marjorie, "my friends and I will be enjoying the liberty that innocence brings."

"Yes, Dr Death, so why don't you go and rot where you belong?" Edna knocked the cigarette out of Dr Christie's hand, stamping it out. "And I'll have you know, this is a no-smoking area."

The four watched the police marching a protesting Dr Christie from the regatta. Marjorie felt a huge sense of satisfaction when she eyed her cousin-in-law.

"Well done, Edna. You cracked the case."

Edna beamed. "We all did."

"But you couldn't resist the 'Dr Death' quip, could you?" said Horace, chortling. Watching him and Edna embark on one of their joint snorting sessions was somehow reassuring and quite enjoyable.

"Why don't you buy me a glass of champagne?" Edna said to Horace.

"You deserve it," he replied.

"Not for me," said Marjorie. "A nice pot of tea will suit me just fine."

"And me," said Frederick.

THIRTY-ONE

As the four friends entered the Stewards' Enclosure for the last day of the regatta, their moods were celebratory. Frederick was happy he would soon see justice done for his old friend. Marjorie, Horace and Edna had agreed they would attend the funeral in Cornwall, which would be the week after they all returned from their various engagements.

Edna was dressed in a beautiful lilac dress with a matching hat for the last day. Horace had bought her the new shoes she'd not stopped mentioning since the bee incident, which she was showing off today. The heels were still too high, in Marjorie's opinion, but they suited her cousin-in-law. Even Frederick had treated himself to a new suit and looked rather dashing in white flannel trousers, a red shirt and a white jacket. His trilby had been replaced by a white boater with a red ribbon, courtesy of Horace who insisted the trilby just wouldn't do for the final day.

After their morning teas and coffees in the Coffee and Ices Garden, they settled down in their designated deckchairs to watch the racing. The weather was on the turn with thundery showers forecast for the next day.

"I'm glad the regatta was this week and not next," said Horace. "The forecast's abysmal.

After enjoying the third race of the morning, Edna nudged Marjorie's arm. "I've just been telling Horace about some of the things on my bucket list."

"Oh?" Marjorie was only half-listening.

"Yeah. Now we've done your posh boat racing thing, it's time to do something for me."

Marjorie turned her head, nervous anticipation filling her stomach. "For someone who wasn't at all keen on posh people racing boats, I'd say you've enjoyed the week more than any of us."

"That may be – apart from the murder – but Horace has agreed to my request."

"Enlighten me."

"A Cornish bus tour. Horace says Faith Weathers is leading one in the near future."

Marjorie felt pleasantly relieved. "That sounds like a safe adventure, and it would be nice to see Faith again."

"I told you she'd go for it," Edna said to Horace.

"I'll check Frederick is in agreement."

"Oh, don't worry about him, Marge. Where you go, he'll follow."

"You had to ruin it, didn't you."

Edna shrugged her shoulders. "I only speak the truth, Marge."

Marjorie ignored her, returning her attention to the sound of oars lapping in the water and cries and cheers from the crowds as the next race neared its end.

They thoroughly enjoyed the morning's racing and the atmosphere in the Luncheon Tent was the best yet. They took their seats and Marjorie felt particularly hungry. Perhaps it was because they were getting the last of the good weather. Or maybe it was that they had nothing else to preoccupy their thoughts.

No, Marjorie thought. *It's because we are together and enjoying each other's company.* The awesome foursome as Faith Weathers had christened them. It was good to have another get-together planned. After all, what could happen on a bus tour around Cornwall?

A LETTER FROM THE AUTHOR

Thank you for reading *Murder at the Regatta*. I hope you enjoyed Lady Marjorie and friends' latest outing.

If you want to hear about all my new releases with Storm Publishing, sign up here:

www.stormpublishing.co/dawn-brookes

And if you want to keep in touch about all my books, and receive bonus content, sign up here:

www.dawnbrookespublishing.com/subscribe

If you enjoyed this book and could spare a few moments to leave a review that would be hugely appreciated. Even a short review can make all the difference in encouraging a reader to discover my books for the first time. Thank you so much.

The Lady Marjorie Snellthorpe Mystery series follows a spirited quartet of octogenarians who prove that age is no barrier to sleuthing. Led by Lady Marjorie Snellthorpe, they bring decades of life experience and distinct social backgrounds to the world of crime-solving.

United by their sharp minds and a shared love for justice, they navigate their differences with humour and heart. Though they may not always agree, when it comes to solving murders, they're an unstoppable force.

I created this series to celebrate the wisdom, humour, and

resilience that come with age, showing that even in their golden years, these four are far from done with adventure.

Thanks again for being part of this amazing journey with me and I hope you'll stay in touch – I have so many more stories and ideas to entertain you with.

Dawn Brookes

- facebook.com/dawnbrookespublishing
- tiktok.com/@dawnbrookesauthor
- youtube.com/dawnbrookespublishing
- bookbub.com/authors/dawn-brookes

ACKNOWLEDGEMENTS

Thank you to my scrutiny team for the suggestions and amendments in the early stages.

Thanks to editor Alison Jack for her fine-tuning of this book.

A special thanks to Naomi Knox and the team at Storm Publishing for their support and for helping to bring the books into the hands of new readers.

Thanks for everyone who has supported me in my author journey so far. I couldn't do it without you!

Printed in Dunstable, United Kingdom